A MOMENT COMES

ALSO BY
JENNIFER BRADBURY

SHIFT

WRAPPED

A MOMENT COMES

JENNIFER BRADBURY

Atheneum Books for Young Readers

NEW YORK LONDON TORONTO SYDNEY NEW DELHI

ATHENEUM BOOKS FOR YOUNG READERS

An imprint of Simon & Schuster Children's Publishing Division

1230 Avenue of the Americas, New York, New York 10020

For information about special discounts for bulk purchases, please contact
Simon & Schuster Special Sales at 1-866-506-1949 or business@simonandschuster.com.

The Simon & Schuster Speakers Bureau can bring authors to your live event.
For more information or to book an event, contact the Simon & Schuster Speakers Bureau
at 1-866-248-3049 or visit our website at www.simonspeakers.com.

The text for this book is set in Janson Text LT.

Manufactured in the United States of America

First Edition

2 4 6 8 10 9 7 5 3 1

Bradbury, Jennifer.

A moment comes / Jennifer Bradbury. — 1st ed.

p. cm.

Summary: As the partition of India nears in 1947 bringing violence even to Jalandhar, Tariq,
a Muslim, finds himself caught between his forbidden interest in Anupreet, a Sikh girl, and
Margaret, a British girl whose affection for him might help with his dream of studying at Oxford.

ISBN 978-1-4169-7876-3 (hardcover) — ISBN 978-1-4169-8302-6 (eBook)

[1. Interpersonal relations—Fiction. 2. Toleration—Fiction. 3. Household employees—Fiction.
4. Family life—India—Fiction. 5. Muslims—Fiction. 6. Sikhs—Fiction.
7. India—History—Partition, 1947—Fiction.] I. Title.

PZ7.B71643Mom 2013

[Fic]—dc23   2012028331

To Robin,
FOR SEEING THE PROMISE,
AND TO Caitlyn,
FOR HELPING IT GET THERE

ACKNOWLEDGMENTS

Thank you to Angie Wright, Laural Ringler, Beth Miller, Julia Mesplay, and June Bradbury for reading, encouraging, and being amazing. Thanks to Mary Beth Conlee, Karen Prasse, and the wonderful staff at the Burlington Public Library for the critiques and the research help. Any errors are my own. Thanks to the Puget Sound Writing Project and Janine Brodine for their tireless support of writers at all ages and stages. Thank you to Neera Puri, Damini Puri, Vineeta Arora, Inderpreet Sahney, Ayushee Arora, Ibadat Sahney, Mrs. Bajwa, Meenakshi Mohindra, and the entire Bhavan Vidyalaya family in Chandigarh for sharing stories, for checking my Punjabi phrases, and for making India like a second home. Thank you also to Namrata Tripathi, for checking my phrasings. Again, any errors are my own. Special thanks to the late Shibani and Captain T. P. Singh. You are missed. Thanks to Donna Booth and Kevin Schubkegel for never minding how I took over the conference room, and to the staff of TLC preschool for helping me carve out time to revise this book. And always, always, always thanks to Jimmy, Evie, and Arun for everything else.

"MEN ARE CRUEL,
BUT MAN IS KIND."

—RABINDRANATH TAGORE

CHAPTER 1

TARIQ

JUNE 3, 1947

"I know you will make us proud, Tariq," Master Ahmed calls out to me as I step onto the dusty sidewalk outside the school gates.

I lift my palm to my face, fingertips to my forehead, bow. "Khuda hafiz."

"And may He guard you as well," Master Ahmed replies. "Give my best to your parents."

"Shukriya."

I speed up as I round the corner with its scrubby cricket pitch. It seems like longer than a year has passed since I sat for my examinations, since I enrolled at the college. Doing nothing has a way of slowing time. The college shut down after the professors got scared and quit teaching, when both the school and the faculty became easy targets for the Sikh mobs. And with no school, with nothing changing but the way people all over Punjab seem to have gone crazy, I've felt stuck. Trapped, even.

But now. Now there is hope.

My hand sneaks into my pocket, just to make sure the slip of paper is still there. I have already memorized the number of the house on Mani Margh, the time of my appointment with this Darnsley man, the few details about the job. I don't need the paper anymore. All the same, I like knowing it's there, like a railway ticket. Proof that I have someplace to be.

Someplace other than Abbu's shops, selling gold and stones.

And maybe, just maybe, someplace other than India altogether.

This Mr. Darnsley *must* have gone to Oxford. Why else would this chance come?

I walk half a mile, rubbing the paper like some kind of talisman, my mind racing ahead to how hard I'll work to impress this Englishman. It's perfect, really, the timing of it all. I'm so lost in my thoughts that I don't notice the crowd of men running up the lane behind me until they overtake and surround me.

I let go of the paper and brace myself for a fight before I see the men are Muslim, most of them around my age. A few wear prayer caps, but there is not a pagri on the head of any of them, and all have hair cropped close like mine. My hands uncurl.

They are not interested in me. Let them pass.

But then one stops a few yards ahead, turns around. "Tariq!"

My hands clench.

"Sameer," I say. Sameer. There's always trouble when Sameer turns up. Even when we were at school together, he had a way of finding trouble, of drawing me into it.

He fights the current of the men, grabs my arm, and pulls me into the flow.

"What's going on?"

"What do you think?" he asks, smiling. He is a little winded. The mob is keeping up a quick pace. There must be twenty or thirty men here.

Up ahead, two of them break off from the pack, dash over to a market stall, and snatch up armfuls of cricket bats. They're already back in step before the shopkeeper even has a chance to say anything. Not that he would. Not that any of the people in the shops would. They have all stopped to watch.

Someone near the front begins the chant. "Pa-ki-stan Zin-da-bad."

The stolen bats begin to filter through the mob, still keeping pace. Sameer hands one to me before taking one for himself.

My gut turns inside out, hollow. I look around for some way to get myself out of here.

"Pa-ki-stan Zin-da-bad."

"I have to get home!" I yell so Sameer can hear me over the chanting.

His face goes hard. "No you don't, brother."

The fellow on Sameer's other side, a giant of a man, with a heavy beard that makes him look even more threatening, leans around to give me a look. A look that dares me to say I need to go home again. I shut my mouth.

I don't know where we're going, or what we're going to do when we get there, apart from the fact that it will be not be good. I've been careful so far. Managed to avoid getting caught up in any of this violence. Allah's teeth! Why today of all days?

Even if I could sneak away, I'm as worried about what Sameer will think of me—what he might say about me—as I am about getting hurt in some brawling.

This is no time to let loyalties be suspected.

Some of the men with bats in their hands have taken to beating the tips against the ground in time with the chant. "Pa-ki-stan Zin-da-bad."

The lane widens, empties into a little cuanka. Across the way, moving in from the other street, another mob is moving in. Bigger than ours.

My grip tightens, and I realize that this is it. I'm going to have to go through with this, just to survive.

But instead of clashing with the other mob, they take up our chant and we merge together, angling south across the square, which is empty now.

"Pa-ki-stan Zin-da-bad." Some fifty voices chant together.

We are heading for the gurdwara, I realize.

The Sikh temple is not the only one in Jalandhar. It is not

the biggest or grandest, either. A single small dome squats in the center of the roof, topped with the gilt khanda, the crossed swords glinting in the morning light. It is nothing fancy compared to the dozens of gurdwaras in town.

But it is the only one that has no outer wall to protect it.

There are still people inside. I can hear the prayers spilling out the windows.

No . . . no . . . I can't do this.

"Pa-ki-stan Zin-da-bad."

I can't . . .

"Ready?" Sameer presses close and asks me.

No. I don't want to be here. I can't be here.

But I manage to nod, even though I know I look as scared as I feel.

Sameer leans around, forces me to look at him as we slow up. He lifts an eyebrow, shakes his head. The same shake he used to give me when we were kids and I wouldn't take him up on a dare.

But he doesn't have time to say anything. The mob abandons the chant and rushes at the whitewashed sides of the building, screaming.

And it begins.

The building is burning before I even see that some of the men have been carrying cans of petrol. But there are people still in there! Maybe kids. Maybe women.

It all happens too fast.

Rocks sail through the windows; glass shatters inward. Rags

soaked in oil and set alight find their way through the holes. But the people inside—

It's a nightmare come to life.

I don't know what to do.

Sameer is gone, joining the attack. I should run now.

Sikh men begin to pour from the building, chased out by the smoke. But as soon as they step outside, someone is there to make sure they don't get far.

The bodies begin to pile up at the entrance without even making it to the street.

There's nothing I can do to stop it. I don't know how to begin to stop it.

The only thing I can do is run before I have to do anything to hurt any of them.

I don't see Sameer. If I go now, he'd never know.

But I've barely taken a step when movement to my right catches my eye. A man, his white pagri already black with smoke, launches himself from one of the broken windows on the ground floor. The fight is centered toward the front of the building. No one is there to meet him when he comes out.

But then he sees me. Me, standing there with a cricket bat outside his temple.

He screams, brandishing a kirpan, the little sword flashing silver in the sunlight.

He rushes at me, the knife tracking straight for my chest. I freeze, but I have to move. Move! Maybe I could knock it from his hand, knock him off balance, give myself time to get away. But what if I miss? What if my timing is off? But I have to try. So I lunge forward, swinging the bat like I have in matches a thousand times before. I swing as hard as I can for his arm. But to my horror I realize he's moving too fast. . . . I'm going to miss his hand . . . and I can't stop.

The end of the bat catches him square on the chin. Blood spits from his mouth as his head snaps sharply back.

He drops at my feet, the knife falling from his slack hand.

I can't move for a second, the impact of the bat jarring through me like an aftershock, the crack of his jaw echoing in my ears. But I am still standing.

The man is completely still. Allah, please, no . . .

He lies facedown in the dirt, blood running from his mouth and chin. No, no, no. I can't have killed him. Can't have. I only meant to keep him from killing me. I didn't mean to—

My stomach retches, and I bend forward, heave into the dirt. My hands are covered with a spray of blood—his blood. I get sick again.

Maybe he isn't dead, I tell myself. *Maybe he'll wake up later. He would've killed me.* And as I think it, I realize someone still might.

I straighten, look up quickly, and ready the bat in case someone else is coming at me. There are bodies all over the courtyard. A pile of them blocks off the front entrance, and the mob I came with has spread itself out, picking off the others coming out the windows now. I don't see any women. Or children. I don't know if it means they're all still trapped inside, or if they just weren't here today. I hope, I *pray* it's the latter.

Just then Sameer sprints by with a couple of other men on their way to the back of the gurdwara, where more must be trying to escape. He catches my eye, glances down at the body at my feet, the bat in my hand, and raises his own bat in salute. He gestures for me to follow before disappearing around the side of the building.

But I don't. I throw the bat down next to the man I hit—the man who hasn't moved, hasn't even stirred. Then I turn and run.

CHAPTER 2

ANUPREET

The seam on my face is healing.

My fingers walk the distance from the bone beneath my eye to the hollow of my cheek. It bubbles and puckers, but it's better than it was before.

"Stop touching it, girl," Biji says without even turning away from the roti puffing on the stove.

Just as I open my mouth to ask how she knew, she tells me.

"I cannot hear the pin moving, which means you've stopped rolling out the chapatis. Get back to work."

I pinch off another chunk of dough, press it down with my hands before finishing it with the pin.

"It will not heal if you worry it so," Biji clucks, flipping the roti on the tawa.

"It is nearly healed," I argue.

Biji clucks again, like an annoyed hen, then draws her hand away quick from the heat and slips it into her mouth. "It will fade more," she says sternly, "if you leave it be and stay out of the sun."

Stay out of the sun. I have not been out of doors since that day three weeks ago. I have scarcely seen sun or another soul outside of Biji, Papaji, and my brother, Manvir. At least I won't be so alone soon.

Biji turns and flips her braid over her shoulder to keep it from the flame. "How many?"

I survey the pile of dough still remaining. "A dozen, I think."

Biji nods. "When your uncle comes"—she sighs—"we will make dozens more. Little ones eat nothing but bread."

I smile at the thought of sharing the house with my youngest cousins.

"Uncle's wife will help," I say.

Biji makes a sound that translates to something like *we'll see about that.* She's never met Uncle's wife or his children. But I can tell by the way she's been busy scaring up extra bedding and studying the arrangement of the three small sleeping rooms in our house that she's excited, too.

All of us will be happier to have the house feel crowded for a while. To have something else to worry over besides my scar or whether it is safe for me to go outside.

I have not returned to school. My teachers have sent lessons home when they could, and Vineeta and Neera have sent me notes tucked inside the packets from time to time, but even those have come less often. It feels as if they are forgetting me. As if I had died.

I am allowed to go to gurdwara, but only with my dupatta pulled low over my face like a veil. And once Biji let me walk to the end of the street, but only because Manvir was with me.

But no going to the market, or anything by myself, since it happened.

I long for the day when Biji sends me to the lane to meet the milk wallah on his motorcycle. I used to hate getting up so early in the morning for the task, but now I can only remember the lovely way the milk flowed into the pot from the ladle, the quiet ticking of the motorbike engine as it cooled while he dipped and poured, dipped and poured.

"Hello?" I hear my father call from the front door of the house.

"Here!" I shout.

Papaji joins us in the small cooking porch. "What smells so good?"

"We're not ready for you," Biji says. "Why so early?"

Papaji hesitates. "Gagandeep closed early. There was some trouble this morning at the gurdwara nearby."

Biji stops. "Trouble?"

Papaji waves her off. "Nothing to worry about," he says. But he's lying. If they shut up the shop early, when every day Papaji talks about how crowded it is . . . Mr. Gagandeep wouldn't give up half a morning's business for nothing.

"Where is Manvir?" Papaji asks.

"Helping Navdeep with his father's roof. He'll be home soon," I say.

My father looks relieved, shoulders falling just a bit. He is tall, still taller than Manvir, whom Biji swears is still growing. But Papaji says his brother, the uncle I have never met, will tower over them both. A single loop of black hair has escaped Papaji's pagri, dipping toward the collar of his white shirt. The creases on his pants are still as sharp as when he left this morning. I should know. I pressed them there.

"Were you busy?" Biji tries to pretend things are normal.

He sighs. "Very. A chemist is always busy. Though fewer come to buy medicines. The Muslims come to buy tooth powders and things they need for their journeys, or things they fear they won't be able to find after they shift west. And those who stay behind, they buy medicine of a different kind."

Biji stiffens.

"And we are out of what they require," he says sadly. "When the tenth man came in requesting cyanide tablets after I'd run dry after the third inquiry—"

"Take the food to the table, Anupreet," my biji breaks in, thrusting a bowl of chana saag at me, the chickpeas studding the spinach like stones in the road.

I take the bowl wordlessly, look to Papaji, who seems able to see only my scar, and slip inside to the table.

Before I am out of earshot, she hisses at him, "Do not speak of such things in front of her!"

"Anupreet is nearly sixteen. She is not a child—"

"And she has the scar to prove it!" Biji shoots back. "Why fill her head with more fear?"

"Does she know what the men want poison for?" Papaji asks.

I want to rush back in and tell them that I do. That Inderpreet showed me the wooden box her father gave her a month ago, the white pill inside. That she should take it if her virtue was threatened—

"She knows enough to stay inside the house!" Biji returns.

"You *keep* her in the house!" Papaji says back quietly.

"For her safety. You saw how men used to look at her—"

Papaji's tone softens, his voice stepping lower. "What happened in the shop that day didn't happen because she is a beauty. She was in the wrong place at the wrong moment."

Biji slams the pot onto the stove. "We live in the wrong moment. All of us. The whole of the Punjab." Her voice fades as I hear the slip of the roti against the tawa, the flip as it settles on its other side.

Papaji is silent a moment.

"She'll die inside this house if we keep her chained up."

"Better than dying in the street," Biji mumbles.

I reenter the kitchen, fetch the pile of roti, and carry it to the table.

After I've gone, I hear Papaji again.

"Maybe there is another way," he says.

I can feel Biji's asking, the question steaming in the air like the puffs that escape from the pinholes in the surface of the bread.

"Mr. Bennet came to see me today," he said.

"The Irishman?"

"He's hiring household staff for a man coming to work on the boundary award."

Biji lets fly a string of oaths. "You want her to work?"

"In a safe place. In a compound. She would live there. Earn some. It will be good for her."

I reappear, feel my biji's eyes on me as I fetch plates and go again. They know I'm listening. They must. I can feel it in the way her eyes watch my movements, then flick nervously to the scar on my cheek.

All the same, they wait until I'm out of sight to continue.

"Where is the house?" Biji asks.

"Near the magistrate."

"The yellow one?"

"Haan," he replies.

"That's a thirty- or forty-minute walk—"

"She'll stay during the week. They will have a room for her. And when Manvinder and his family come, we will need the space," he says, adding quietly, "and the money. Until he finds work."

"But she'll still have to get there—"

"Manvir will fetch her back and forth."

"What will she do for these people?" Biji asks, her resolve weakening.

"A bit of everything. She might work in the kitchen some. Bennet said there is a wife who will need a ladies' maid of sorts. And a daughter who will need Anu's help as well."

Biji sucks air past her teeth. "British girls—they are a bad influence. Not at all respectable—"

I enter on this note and stand perfectly still. There is no more food to bring to the table.

Papaji looks at me and winks. Biji shakes her head as if she knows she is already beaten. I hear the front door open and slam back shut. Manvir is home.

"Go and tell your brother to wash for table," Biji orders me. But I don't go yet. I have to see what Biji says. A job? A fine big house? A girl all the way from England?

"Please, Biji," I beg. "Please let me."

She turns to my papaji. "And what will I do without her here?"

Papaji winks at me. "You'll put my brother's wife to work, I expect."

Biji rolls her eyes, Papaji laughs, and I disappear into the house, the smile breaking across my face, the scar pulling thin across the surface of my cheek.

CHAPTER 3

TARIQ

The stink of the smoke follows me home.

I can't stop shaking, can't stop looking behind me, can't stop seeing the face of that man as the bat connected with his jaw.

My fingers won't stop trembling and I can't get them to open the damn latch on the gate. It's as if my hands don't belong to me. Don't fit with the rest of me.

I finally manage to pry the latch free and get inside the yard. I'm so keyed up, I slam the gate shut without meaning to. It clangs hard and loud like a bell.

"Tariq," I hear my brother call from the rooftop. "Get up here."

I can't face my parents now, anyway. I go to the drainpipe that Arish showed me how to climb when I was little and shimmy up, hand over hand, my toes finding holds in the brackets bolted to the wall. When I pull myself onto the roof, my brother is there, leaning forward on the bench, both hands resting on the top of his cane, his chin on his hands, looking out over the city. Like always.

I join Arish on the bench. He exhales slowly, holds a cigarette out to me without taking his eyes off the smoke billowing in the distance. I don't smoke much—too expensive when I'm trying to put money aside. But I'm glad for the offer now, pulling deep on the sigarata, letting it settle me down. I hold the smoke in my lungs, slow my heart down before I exhale slowly, and hand the cigarette back to Arish.

"They've only just told us that there will be separate states," he says, "and already it's getting worse."

"Haan," I agree, but I'm in no mood to hear his diatribe on how India will be ripped apart to create a second country, to be called Pakistan. I can't stop seeing that man's face snapping back . . . how quickly he fell.

"I have seen war, little brother," Arish says. He is only three years older than me, and I am taller, but he has earned the right to call me what he likes. "And that"—he jabs the cigarette at the fire—"that is the promise of things just starting."

Arish fought for the British in Africa, chasing down Germans in Tunisia. He enlisted in the special corps of Indian soldiers when he was the same age I am now, eighteen. Most of them were Sikhs—but my brother didn't care. Nobody cared much back then.

He came back two years later, half his right leg chewed off in the caterpillar tracks of the German panzer his commanding officer ordered him to attack with his battalion.

I reach for the cigarette and take another drag. I'm not sure if it's the smoke or just listening to my brother, but I'm starting to settle down. "It's going to get worse," he warns, and of course he is right. Our mosque is always full now, not just at prayer times. Men sit and work themselves up over the injustices Muslims suffer, or speak reverently about how wonderful it will be when Pakistan is born, when we have a Muslim state.

I've sat on the fringes of these meetings. Many times. And it's awful to say, but I can't get myself worked up like the others do. I don't care the way I'm supposed to.

I feel guilty for it, but here it is all the same. I don't feel a part of it, don't feel like I belong. Not when what I want is in England. At least in the short term.

"Already they worry whether Lahore will go to Pakistan or stay with India," Arish says, shaking his head, finishing off the cigarette. "As if worrying will change what the budhoo British decide."

"Amritsar, too," I add.

He hisses, flicks the butt off the rooftop. "The viceroy promises all will be settled as soon as August." He scratches at the stump of his leg. "Two months to divide a country and move how many lakhs of people . . ."

The Sikhs to India, the Muslims to Pakistan. But I will not go to Pakistan. Not until I'm ready.

"So . . . ," Arish begins, turning toward me, "what did the schoolmaster—?" He stops, grabs my wrist. "Is that blood?" He rubs at the dried flecks with his thumb. "What happened?"

I nod at the fire in the distance.

"You were there?" he asks. I avoid his eyes. I don't want to tell him. Telling him would only make it more real.

"I left Master Ahmed and the school." I fight to keep my voice even. "A mob caught me up. Sameer was there."

"Are you hurt?" he asks.

I stare at the rooftop a long time before answering.

"Nahi."

"Sameer?" he asks.

I study our feet. My two, dusty from the road, his one, the toes curling around the end of his cane. "I left before it finished."

"Before what finished?" he demands. But I can't talk about it. Can't think about it.

"Master Ahmed has a job for me," I blurt out.

Arish hesitates before he gives in. "Job?" he asks, adding, "now?"

"A new Englishman has come to Jalandhar."

He curses. "Just what we need. More British in India."

"He is a cartographer. Making maps of the boundary award. He needs help."

"What kind of help?" he asks.

"Translating, courier duties, things like that."

He snorts. "My little brother playing Batman to a sahib."

— 19 —

I can't tell if he's serious or not. But I don't care. I need this job.

"Will Abbu let me do it?" I ask, careful not to sound too eager.

"Abbu will allow it," Arish says, smirking. "Daadaa would have loved it."

I thought the same when Master Ahmed told me he'd put me forward for the job. Our great-grandfather had been a member of the viceroy's staff in his day, and Daadaa liked to go on about the proud tradition of "fine Muslim families serving as the wise right hand to the British Raj." It was Daadaa who first told me about the place that to him was almost as holy as Mecca.

Oxford.

All the great men his father worked for, and who he himself worked for later as a civil servant, were educated at Oxford. It was Daadaa who made me believe that I could go there. He'd once tried to persuade my father to consider going himself, but Abbu was too practical for it. He was happy to take the shops that came his way when he married my mother and get busy making his fortune. And then when Arish showed no talent for school and enlisted in the army, Daadaa transferred his hopes to me. I was glad to oblige him.

Before his death, he told Abbu to take a portion of the inheritance he would be leaving behind and set it aside for my education. The rest was up to me.

I did my part. I was the best student the school had ever seen. I stayed out of trouble. It was easy.

But somewhere along the way, what began as a way to please my daadaa, and then to honor his memory after he died, shifted into something else.

It started when Arish came home wounded.

I was angry for my brother. And angry *at* him for letting himself be used, letting himself be shot up in a war that had nothing to do with us in the first place.

I swore I'd never let anything like it happen to me.

And going to Oxford would help make sure it didn't.

After all, the men who'd finally convinced the British to leave—Gandhi, Nehru, Jinnah—all of them were educated in England. No one told *them* what to do. No one told them to throw themselves on top of German tanks. No—Gandhi, Nehru, Jinnah—*they* told an empire to quit India, and it did.

Everyone listened to them. Everyone listens to the men who have the right education from the right places.

I would be one of those men.

But Daadaa had been wrong about one thing. Being smart wasn't enough. Hard work and not getting in trouble and impressing everybody wasn't enough. I found that out after my first six letters to the school went unanswered. Nobody cared about my nearly perfect marks or how my maths teacher kept having to send away for more calculus books because I'd already mastered all the ones he owned.

None of that mattered without connections.

I couldn't simply turn up on the campus and expect to be let in. Not without someone who would give a reference for me. I had to have the right person—someone who'd been there—to convince them to give me a chance. And I didn't have anybody like that. All the men Daadaa used to work with and admire had left India years ago. I was out of luck.

Until now.

"You'll be finished working for him before we have to shift west?" my brother asks.

I hesitate. It's too soon to tell Arish what I'm hoping the job might lead to. "I should. He is only coming to do something with the partition."

He studies me carefully. I start to panic that he's guessed why I'm so game to take the job at a time when I should be helping us get ready to move. What if he tells Abbu before I'm ready? Before I've had a chance to work it all out?

But he surprises me.

"You should take the position . . . ," he begins, but the door leading to the stairs opens abruptly. Abbu appears there, wheezing as he leans heavily against the block wall.

"Sons," he says, gasping, winded by the climb, "come down for prayers."

Arish and I exchange a look. Father often skipped the midday prayer, but the day's events—and maybe Ammi's badgering—must have convinced him that today is a good day to be devout.

"Chalo," he orders, heading back down, one hand trailing on the wall as he disappears. The servant boy, Ajay, steps silently into view, waiting. Arish rages against the way Ammi treats him like a cripple and refuses to allow himself to be carried up and down the stairs as she wishes. But she makes Ajay walk two steps in front of my brother, ready to catch him should he miss a step.

"Wash your hands before you come down." Arish nods toward the inch or two of rainwater standing in an empty flower pot near our feet. "I'll go extra slow to give you time." He reaches out and touches my shoulder lightly before starting his long hobble-swing across the roof to the stairs.

I pour some of the water from the pot onto my hands and scrub away the bits of dried blood. I roll my sleeves up to cover the stains of the drops that landed on the cuffs. Then I cup the water in my hands and scrub at my face, my eyes, the back of my neck.

When my eyes shut, I see him, see his head snap back, see the blood spray up again.

I might have killed a man. Me. Killed a man. It doesn't seem possible.

Maybe I am just like everybody else. Another Muslim killing another Sikh?

Allah, how did this happen? Why?

But then another thought strikes me.

What if he isn't dead? What if he comes looking for me?

Jalandhar isn't so large a city. Not big enough to hide in forever. If he's still out there . . .

I don't know which possibility is worse. That I accidentally killed him, or that I didn't.

And I realize that now I have another reason to leave India to add to my list.

CHAPTER 4

MARGARET

It's ruddy hot.

The car bumps along through what passes here for a street, dipping and jostling every few feet with whatever hole catches a wheel. And that's when we're moving at all. Most of the time we sit here idling as we wait for the road to clear out some so we can inch forward a bit. Sometimes we're waiting for a skinny rat of a dog or even a cow to clear out. *Cows.* Back home if there had been a cow on the loose in London, I reckon half the coppers would have been after it, but here nobody pays them any mind.

And when we're not waiting for the animals to decide to shove off, there are the packs and packs of people. They walk up the middle of the lanes as though they aren't expecting cars to come along, or crash into one another with their bicycles and motorbikes, and stand there having a row about it like we aren't even waiting to get by. Of course, the longer we sit, the longer people have to gather and stare into the car, pointing at us, smiling to one another.

At least the cows and the dogs don't stare.

The heat inside the car is oppressive, but it's nothing compared to all those brown faces, the inkwell eyes staring at me through the glass of the windows. Mouths hanging open, baskets tilting off their heads, grips slackening on parcels. But I don't dare roll down my window for the little hands of the beggar children that tap on the glass.

Only the driver has his window down, so he can lean out and shout at the people or animals ignoring the blaring of his horn. I've been in Jalandhar half an hour and already he's used the blasted instrument more times than I've heard it total at home in England.

And it's just as well the other windows are up. Opening them might bring some fresh air, but most certainly would mean more of that smell.

Like a barn and a latrine all at once. But oilier. Spicier. Hotter.

"You shouldn't have made me come," I say to Mother for the hundredth time.

She sighs, breathing out slowly, like an actress preparing to step on stage. We both know this script. But this time she doesn't rise to the bait.

She doesn't remind me again what an opportunity India

represents for all of us. Mummy likes to make it sound as if Daddy's saving the world down here, one of the only cartographers the viceroy, Lord Mountbatten, brought down to help break India into pieces so the Muslims can have their separate state. I'm sure Daddy's work is very important and all, but it's got nothing to do with me, that part.

It was the newspapers that did me in. All the papers back in London with those photographs of Lady Mountbatten and her daughter, Pamela, hoofing it around refugee camps, dining with dignitaries on both sides, even Gandhi himself, the man everybody said almost single-handedly got the British to agree to quit India in the first place.

Before they came to India, and started turning up in the dailies back home, the Mountbattens weren't much. Lord Mountbatten was a cousin or something of the king, and they were great pals in the bargain, but he was just an admiral in the Royal Navy. And by all accounts, he wasn't much of an officer, either. Churchill apparently thought him a complete duffer, but the king decided when it was time for the empire to wash its hands of the crown jewel and that Lord Mountbatten was just the man for the job. Most of the world reckoned the king had just picked a suitable scapegoat, someone Jinnah, the Muslim firebrand, and Nehru, the Congress Party leader of India, could railroad. That way, when everything went south, they'd have no one to blame but themselves.

But Mountbatten had other ideas. He took the job of

dividing India so seriously that he became something of a hero, even if the job itself was next to impossible.

The fact that he brought his glamorous wife and his nineteen-year-old daughter along with him for the job only made him more popular. Lady Mountbatten and Pamela were always about helping, looking useful. They'd become even more popular at home than before. Perfect celebrities, really.

And as soon as they became so dead famous, Mummy took to calling on some terribly convoluted connection between our families to anyone who cared to listen. I'm not sure how distantly related we are to the Mountbattens—far enough that Mother doesn't bother trying to explain to people the connection, preferring instead that they imagine we're twin branches on the same tree rather than an acorn that fell away and grew into its own scraggly oak. But to hear Mother speak of it, we're great chums, Pamela and I, though I've never met her and Mother's certainly never met Lord or Lady Mountbatten. And we're not likely to while we're here. Daddy's working here in Jalandhar, hours north of Delhi, where Mountbatten is set up. And we won't exactly be rubbing elbows with Lady E. and Cousin Pammie, I expect.

But to Mother, that detail is totally unimportant. The fact that we'll return to England with the same sun on our skin, the same glow of importance . . . that's what she's after.

"The experience will elevate us," Mother says coolly, breaking her silence as the driver swerves to avoid a bicycle with a basket of live chickens mounted behind the seat.

I snort. "If you wanted me elevated, I could have stayed home and ridden the lift in Harrods all day." But I know what she really means.

What she means is it will make them all forget.

Forget him. And me. Us.

Alec.

I want to say his name out loud, whisper it the way I did sometimes in the dark in my dormitory back at boarding school—where Mother sent me after she found out about us. But I don't. Don't want to give her a chance to say the things she always says about him if I bring him up. That he was a soldier of no birth or connection, an American, for God's sake. A rogue almost ten years my senior who had designs on ruining my virtue and my family's reputation, and blackmailing Daddy in the bargain.

The only parts Mother ever gets right are that he was American and he was twenty-five.

Alec was a hero. He took shrapnel in his leg when he was manning a machine gun at Bastogne, but he kept his post, kept firing, kept the other men in his unit alive. When he came to the ward where I volunteered, they'd just given him medals for valor and for being wounded. He was shy and quiet and kind and still having nightmares about the war. I used to sit up with him talking. We became friends. And then more.

The day he walked for the first time without his crutch was the day he told me he loved me.

He *loved* me.

But then Mother found out. She didn't believe we were really in love. I was sixteen. What could I understand about love, yet? They packed me off to boarding school the next week, and I never saw Alec again.

When I got back from boarding school for the summer holiday, she gave me a letter that had been waiting there for me for the last two months.

I remember seizing it, running up to my room. I savored every word until I got to the bit where he told me about how he'd met a girl back in Pennsylvania and he was very sorry but my parents made it clear that he was not welcome.

Mother announced the next day that she'd decided we'd join Daddy for the last couple of months of his service in India. She hadn't even considered coming with Daddy when he first got the appointment to work on the boundary award—hardly any of the other men who'd been brought down had their families along—but when the papers back home started featuring Lady Edwina and Cousin Pammie looking noble and selfless every day as they slummed it down in India, Mother must have hatched her plan. Said it would be wonderful to be together, wonderful to have a chance to expand my horizons.

Then I was too heartbroken to argue with her. But now. Now. This place. What am I doing here?

I lean down and mop my forehead with the skirt of my dress. "I don't know how my perspiring to death in a country the empire is soon to wash its hands of will do the trick of making me virtuous again."

She eyes the damp patch near my hem with contempt. "I don't suppose you do."

The car lurches to a halt, our driver exiting this time to gesture and shout at a man pulling a cart laden with what look like bed frames. As the car idles, I hear a bit of music, almost sounding like an organ. I look around, but can't tell where it's coming from. The tune hums and calls, some kind of drum providing rhythm beneath the melody. I find myself suddenly eager for a piano, wondering if I can copy the notes.

The driver hops back into his seat. He's spied an open track on the road, and he speeds for it with abandon, horn blaring. Soon we're clearing our way of the town proper, the houses spreading out a bit. Mother's barmy. But I don't say so out loud in case the driver's English is better than he let on when he collected us on the platform. Plus, I've said it before. It didn't do any good then, either.

Bells, I want a cigarette. Just to smell something other than the stinking air in the car. But that wouldn't do. Not with Mother right next to me. She's been campaigning since I got back from school to have me give them up, even though she smokes a few a day too. But it's different for me. She doesn't want people seeing me smoking, doing something adult because she reckons it puts them in mind of the other adult things I've done.

Instead she wants people seeing me sweating like a scrubber

in church, spooning gruel into some refugee's cup. Because that'll make me respectable again.

The car slows as we turn and drive through an open iron gate, flanked by walls as yellow as the sun in a child's painting. I almost have to look away.

We slide to a stop, and I look through the window and the cloud of dust kicked up by the tires to study my new home. The building is painted a version of the yellow on the high walls surrounding the compound, but faded and peeling in spots. I can see where someone has come round with a brush recently and tried to touch it up in places, but the new paint on top of the old is so much brighter that it does more to shine a light on the bad patches than it does to cover them up. The facade is broken by a wide veranda on the second floor. Screens stretch across all the windows. White gables around the columns reveal more cracks in the paint like lacy spiderwebs. The dusty gravel driveway fades into a scrub of baked brown grass that presses up against the interior walls. It might have been a grand house once, but something about it has given up.

Father opens my door.

"Meggie!" he cries, pulling me from the car, folding me in his arms, uncharacteristically enthusiastic in his embrace. He's been lonely for us, I suppose.

He lets me go, rushes to the other side to meet Mother. They stand there a moment, almost unsure. Father is tall, his sandy hair thinning at the front but still wavy along the sides. His blue eyes squint against the low sun as he looks at my mother, just a tick shorter than he is, her brown eyes and hair the closest any of us might come to fitting in here in India.

She reaches for his hand, takes it, and he pulls her the rest of the way in, kissing her full on the cheek. Honestly.

"There's your room there, love," Father says to me, pointing at the window on the second floor opposite the verandah.

I look up, shade my eyes. "Can the piano be moved in there for me?"

Father's mouth drops open a bit before he turns and says to Mother, "I thought you told her."

She gives him a look that says she had a hard enough time getting me here at all.

"Told me what?" I ask.

"Well . . . ," Father begins, "there is no piano. . . ." He drones on a bit about how awfully expensive they are, how they don't abide the heat, how they couldn't get one no matter how hard they tried and, besides, I'll only be here a couple of months . . .

But all I hear is *no piano*.

Of course there isn't.

I'm about to argue back that they can't bring me halfway round the world *and* not provide me a piano. But then I realize that what must be the household staff has assembled to greet us on the drive.

A household staff of precisely four people.

There is a girl about my age whom I almost miss because she's lingering in the shadows of the main entrance. Even in the dim, I can tell I'm in the presence of a girl far prettier than I am. A girl who doesn't stoop to hide her height like I do, a girl whose features aren't as sharp as mine.

She is beautiful, and I fight the instant flash of resentment clawing its way up my spine.

Next to her is a woman who looks twice as old as my mother, a woman whose demeanor and stance and clothing telegraph her existence as the housekeeper of this place.

And beside her, a man who fits so perfectly with her that he can only be her husband. A matched set.

But fetching the bags from the boot of the car is someone who belongs to no one.

A young bloke. My age. With the same dark skin and hair I've seen everywhere. But his eyes, his eyes are something like amber. He lifts the trunk like it's nothing and starts toward the house.

He's deadly good-looking, this one.

A little something stirs and stretches in my belly. And it dawns on me that maybe India won't be so terrible after all.

CHAPTER 5

TARIQ

Darnsley's daughter brought more items with her than I own. I carried everything from the car to the second floor and her bedroom. By the time I finished, the bed had all but disappeared behind a collection of trunks, three hatboxes, and an old leather portfolio, its corners peeling back to reveal sheet music. When I collected the last of her things, she told her parents she was going to look at the room and started up the stairs ahead of me.

She's tall. Almost as tall as me. And her hair is bright and sort of yellow. She's pretty, I guess, in the way white women are. And I have to keep myself from staring at her legs. They're great, the part I can see sticking out below the bottom of her skirt. But they're strange, too, the way I can see the faint line of the blue blood vessel running up her calf. She'll take some getting used to.

She points across the hall when we get to the top of the stairs. I nod, let her lead the way into her room.

"Cozy," she says, looking around.

"Anything more, miss?" I ask, placing the box on the floor with the others.

She doesn't answer, turning toward me, crossing her arms, and tilting her head to one side. Now it's her turn to size me up. Only she's even bolder about it than I was on the stairs. I don't like it. It feels too much like when I walk by a group of women and they whisper to one another and laugh after I pass.

"Whatsat?" she asks after too long. Her English is a wreck. The words are right, but the way she throws them out is all wrong. So the fact that she cannot understand me, with the accent I have worked so hard to perfect, irritates me.

"Anything more, miss?" I flatten out the syllables that are necessary in Punjabi but sound singsong when they creep into English.

"I'm Margaret," she offers. "What're you called?"

She's toying with me. A cat with a mouse.

"Tariq," I tell her.

She straightens her shoulders, lifts her chin. "Tah-reek," she says, exaggerating the sounds. "Thanks ever, Tah-reek." And she grins.

Bakavasa. This could be trouble. *She* could be trouble.

I bow slightly, turn on my heel, and slip out of the room, pulling the door shut behind me as I retreat. My mind is reeling.

I have too golden an opportunity here to let anything get in the way. Everything depends on Mr. Darnsley's satisfaction with me.

So far I have found my new employer easy enough to please. In the three weeks I have worked for him, I've unpacked crates and boxes, helped organize a schedule for his work, translated for him when he had need, and fetched messages back and forth to the telegraph office. He seems happy with my work.

It's been easy. Like school. They made me head boy my last year. All I had to do was do whatever the teachers wanted before they asked, and do it better than anybody else. And here, there is no one to compete with like there had been at school.

But at school there were no girls. No girls to distract me or complicate things.

And in this house, there are two.

Margaret. Margaret I didn't bargain for. I have to step lightly with that one.

But Anupreet.

Anupreet.

She is the most beautiful girl I have ever seen. Even with that scar, or maybe because of it. Something about it makes her mysterious. Like she has a story that I wish I knew. Already I find myself inventing reasons to go below stairs, just to have a look at her. The other employees—especially the cook and her husband—give me the evil eye whenever I come close. Of course they do. She is Sikh. It didn't matter before. Sikhs and

Muslims even married sometimes. But not anymore. Not since this started, and everyone began worrying about who was going to get what if India got split up.

It's just as well. I can't afford the distraction if I'm going to make it to England. All the same, I can't get her out of my head. I go to Darnsley's study and am surprised to find him back at his desk so soon after his family's arrival.

"Tariq?" Mr. Darnsley looks up from his blotter, then reaches for one of the envelopes I stacked in the tray.

I move to the desk and stand ready.

"Take this note to the post." He scrawls an address on the outside of the envelope, and I see that it is bound for New Delhi and Lord Mountbatten. He dumps a handful of coins into my palm.

"Not the telegraph office?" I ask.

He sighs. "I'm afraid not. It is not official. My wife . . . She asked that I—" He stops himself as if he suddenly recalls to whom he is speaking. "It's not important. Nor is the speed with which it makes its way to New Delhi. Only the fact that I have fulfilled this obligation is of any import."

I return half the money he gave me. "This is enough, sir," I say, shaking the remaining paisa in my hand. He looks at me approvingly. I could have pocketed the extra money and he'd never have known the difference. He knows it too.

"Thank you, Tariq," he says. "Now be off with it before that woman can ask me about it again. She's only been here an hour, but I know I won't have a moment's peace until the letter has left my desk."

I go downstairs, head outside, and grab the bicycle from behind the house. Pulling the leather satchel from the basket, I slide the envelope inside and throw the satchel over my shoulder. The guard doesn't even look at me as I push the bicycle to the front. He tugs the gate open, barely waiting long enough for me to get through before shutting it behind me. He does not like me. None of them do. I am the only Muslim working in the house. It makes me easy to dislike.

I wheel to the street, glad to be out of doors, glad to be doing something other than moving that girl's luggage.

"Your fancy white employer hasn't given you a car?" Sameer calls from behind me as I sling my leg over the bicycle.

Sameer. The last person I want to see. My whole body goes tense. Taking a deep breath, I face him. "What are you doing here?" My grip tightens on the leather courier pouch strapped to my chest.

He has a cut across his temple—nearly healed—that he might have gotten after I left the riot. But the skin beneath his left eye is purple and yellow with a fresh bruise. He's been busy since then.

"You're the empire's man now, are you?" he says, ignoring my question, a smirk that is hinting insult across his face.

"I am no one's man," I say, placing a foot on the pedal. "But I am in a hurry."

He laughs. "Of course you are. Ferrying their notes across the city like a good little boy—"

"It is *work*," I spit out, adding, "something you should try."

The grin falters a bit. Sameer's family is poor. Abbu says it's because Sameer's father is too proud to work at a job he thinks beneath him. Sameer recovers, but he wags a finger at me. "Tariq." He shakes his head. "Is that any way to greet an old friend?"

We're not friends. We never were. Friends have things in common. Things other than the few afternoons we spent as boys looking for something to do, waiting for something to happen.

"Did you need something?" I ask, reasoning there's little chance Sameer would make the two miles from our neighborhood to Darnsley's compound for nothing.

He smiles again, the motion pulling the wound at his temple. The smile shifts into a wince. He reaches up to touch it. "Got this that day at the gurdwara."

He pauses, looks me up and down. "I lost you in the crowd, but you're no worse for the wear, are you? And you got the better of at least one of those kuthas."

I don't respond, but I feel the wave of nausea that hits every time I think of the man, the one I hit.

"How are you getting on with your little job? What does he have you doing for him, this great sahib?"

I square my foot on the pedal, lean over the handlebars, but still I do not go. "I serve as Mr. Darnsley's secretary." The title is one of my own making, and maybe a bit overdone, but how will Sameer ever know? "I am a courier and translator. And he works for Radcliffe, who is determining the boundaries, the borders themselves." I know I stand a bit taller as I say this, but I cannot help gloating.

But before the words even finish leaving my mouth, I realize my mistake. Chutiyaa.

Sameer came here for a purpose. And something about his expression now tells me that I have accomplished it for him.

"Then you are a prince among us indeed." He bends slightly at the waist as if to bow. "Fetching papers and teaching Punjabi to a Britisher who will never leave his compound—"

I know I should keep my mouth shut—*shut!*—but still I cannot stop myself. "He goes out. We go on a surveying trip next month."

The smile again. And I hate that Sameer apparently knows me well enough that he can coax information from me with simple taunts.

I hate him.

"A man of the people," he says then, with mock surprise. "No wonder you're so eager to do his bidding—"

"It is work," I manage, "no more."

The smile vanishes slowly, like mist off the hills. Now he is serious. Now he is staring at me fully.

"Work is good," he says carefully, "but it is even better that this man is nothing but an employer to you. That your position is nothing but a means to an end."

"Sameer—"

"Because we have ends as well."

We?

"And should you find yourself with an opportunity to serve the cause of the oppressed Muslim—"

"I have to go," I say, cutting him off. I can't listen to this anymore. I've heard it all before from the men who fume inside the mosque, the same men who rile up crowds in the streets, arm them with clubs and knives and then lead them into Hindu or Sikh neighborhoods. I don't need to hear it from the likes of Sameer.

I turn, push down hard on the pedal, and ride fast up the lane.

His voice calls out after me. "You are one of us, Tariq," he reminds me, adding, "and I know you'll remember that."

CHAPTER 6

ANUPREET

"I don't like that boy," Manvir says when he comes to collect me for my first Sunday off.

Tariq sits in the shade of the wall mending a puncture on his bicycle tire.

"He doesn't speak to me," I reply. Which is true. He tried once, early on, but Shibani and her husband sort of shooed him away, like a chicken that had wandered from the yard into the house. But he doesn't speak much to anyone, really. Tariq is careful with his words, counting them out the way a banker watches coins. He spends each one carefully. And he hadn't wasted any on me.

Manvir grunts as if this is the only way a Muslim and a Sikh could breathe the same air, by pretending the other did not exist, but still he frowns.

"He looks at you," my brother says, turning full round, stopping to glare hard at Tariq.

"You think everyone looks at me," I say, pulling at his arm before Tariq can read the fire in my brother's eyes.

"Everyone does."

He had been looking at me, but not the way Manvir thinks. I've caught Tariq sometimes from a window, or waiting near the kitchen. I think maybe he is lonely, like me, and wants someone to talk to. I feel bad that Shibani and her husband chased him off those times. He only needs a friend.

Besides, Manvir is wrong. If my brother could see Margaret with her yellow hair, he'd know how wrong he is. Why would anyone think I'm pretty with Margaret around? But I'm tired of fighting with him about it, so I change the subject.

"They have rooms for everything!" I gush to Manvir as he exchanges sat sri akals with the porter who holds the gate open for us. "There's even a room for Mrs. Darnsley to get dressed in. Just for her dressing! Can you imagine? A whole room for clothing and powders and perfumes and no bedroll on the floor?"

"And you've your own room in which to sleep?" he asks.

"Yes," I say. "In the attic. There are two beds. The housekeeper and her husband were meant to stay up there, but he can't climb the stairs, so they sleep in the room near the kitchen that was meant for me." I stop short of telling him that I've slept in both beds, just for the joy of being able to choose. Sometimes I wake in the middle of the night and climb into the other bed just to feel the coolness of the sheets against my legs, just because I can. I don't mind at all having to make two beds in the morning.

I check his expression, see the clouds forming there. I've said too much. My brother, after all, is still living in our little rented house soon to be crammed even more full.

"I'm sorry, Manvir," I whisper as he pulls me into the street. "It was thoughtless of me—"

He stops, looking both ways up the crowded margh. Then he looks at me.

"What did you say?" But there is no malice in his tone. No resentment.

I hesitate. "I should not have boasted about the house when you—"

He waves my concern away. "I am not cross with you, Anupreet," he says, eyes flicking away from mine to a pack of young men across the road. "I'm distracted. Too many things to think on."

"Then let me use my paisa to hire a rickshaw wallah," I protest again. "I have enough to get us home and—"

"We need as much as you can give us for the household, sister," he says, avoiding my eyes.

I look down, ashamed at having wanted to return home in a rickshaw when Biji is stretching the chapatis out thinner and thinner every day. But I can't help it. I have never earned money before. The urge to spend some of it tugs at me.

"This way," he says under his breath, steering me toward the center of town instead of toward the school and home.

"Where are we going?" I ask.

He hesitates. "Home."

"But why—" I point at the route that we took last week when Papaji brought me, the quicker way.

"It isn't safe now, Anu," Manvir says quietly. And suddenly I understand why his eyes are shifting around, dancing across the streets and the shop windows like a mongoose before it strikes at a snake. He's afraid.

"Why?"

He avoids my eyes. "There is a Muslim neighborhood two streets over from the school—"

"I know," I say. "But there was a Muslim neighborhood there last week, and the week before that. It's been there since before we were born—"

"A man was beaten to death there two days ago. A Hindu."

I go silent as he pulls me across the road, weaving between bullock carts, waving off rickshaw drivers.

"All over the city," he says almost in a whisper when we reach the other side, "it's getting worse. You remember my friend from school, Aryan?"

I nod.

"He was attacked last week. His mouth gagged with the scraps of his pagri and his hair cut off."

I stop short. "Is he all right?"

Manvir nods. "But he is angry and humiliated. And it won't be long before even good, peaceful men can take no more."

"You wouldn't—"

He steers us around a heap of steaming dung, the straw bristling from its surface. "I would do my duty."

Duty. It seems such an old word, trotted out again now to rally my brother and other mudas like him. Long ago, that duty was sacred. We Sikhs were trusted to protect our Hindu brothers and sisters against the Moghuls and Islam. Guru Gobind Singh raised the army to protect against invading Muslims.

It was so long ago. Hundreds of years have passed. Hindu families stopped giving their eldest sons to the Sikh faith just to bolster the army, as they used to. There was no need.

Sikhs and Muslims were mostly friendly, some even married each other. But then it all changed when the British said they would leave. And there were more of us than there were of them, so the Muslim leaders always made noise about not being treated fairly. But that was only politics.

Until it wasn't.

Overnight, things changed. It was like monkeys and birds who'd been living in the same trees suddenly deciding that wouldn't do anymore and started eating one another.

I grew scared. Going to gurdwara wasn't peaceful anymore. Now we hurried through the songs and prayers so all the men could gather after worship and talk about *duty* again. And it wasn't just in Jalandhar that things got bad. All through the

Punjab, even as far as Bengal in the east, where even Ghandiji's fasts could no longer keep the Muslims and Hindus from killing one another. Duty? What kind of duty was killing?

No. I don't like to hear my brother talk of duty.

Manvir glances behind us for the second or third time since we left the main square.

Before he can stop me, I too look back. And I see what worries him now.

A group of boys—most younger than Manvir—are following us. They catch my eye. The one at the front points, turns to his fellows, and says something that draws laughter from their ranks.

"Who are they?"

Manvir shakes his head. "I saw them only when we passed the tobacco shop."

But I realize with alarm that I had. One or two of the faces are ones I've seen lingering near the compound. And even if all the faces aren't familiar, the shape of the boys is.

A pack always looks the same.

"Why are they following?"

Manvir doesn't answer. Instead he pulls me quickly sideways into the market stalls and we begin to run, taking a right at the first lane, then a left at the next.

"Cover your hair," he orders, checking to see if the boys are still following.

I obey, pulling my dupatta around my head, my heart pounding now.

"What do they want?" I ask.

He doesn't answer, steering us through the maze of vendors.

I thought the scar might have stopped the stares. Or at least drawn them for another reason.

We fly past the bangle seller. Then through clouds of greasy air spilling out of the samosa stand, and on and on, until we emerge on the other side of the market, breathless. Still we run until we make it to the safety of the lanes across the wide expanse of Chandi Margh.

Until we are sure they are not following us anymore.

We slow to a walk. I fight to catch my breath. I'm afraid of the attention we might be drawing. People watch when you run. They watch to see what you're running from. Running to.

"I'd have fought them, you know." Manvir is seething. "I'm sick of running. Sick of it." He kicks a cup dropped from the chai wallah's cart hard, sending it shattering against the wall.

Would he? If I hadn't been here? All of them? And what if they had run us down? Who would have caught the worst of it? Me or Manvir?

"They're gone now, anyway," Manvir says, taking one last long look behind us. "We're safe."

Safe. I think about the word as we continue walking. What does *safe* mean anymore? I wonder if I'll ever feel safe again. I wandered these markets and streets freely just a few years ago.

And then I grew up.

I didn't even notice until Biji began looking at me, by

turns with pride and regret. That was how I knew I was pretty.

And when the men began to stare, that's when I knew it was a problem. When Papaji began trying to put a few more pieces of jewelry aside in the hiding place at home, bangles of thinnest gold, but gold nonetheless, hoping he might have enough to make me a suitable dowry. I began to work even harder at my lessons, perfected my stitches, hopeful someone might notice me for something other than my face.

Manvir suddenly pulls me close. "Biji's right that it's a crime," he's saying, scowling at a man leering at me from an open doorway.

"What crime?" I ask, looking hurriedly away.

"That God make a child both pretty and poor," he says, sending his voice high and reproachful like Biji's scold.

I laugh; he clucks like Biji does.

"But he also made me swift," I say, feeling to urge to run again. "And he gave me a brother to watch out for me."

His expression darkens. "I should have been there that day," he says, angry. "That cur wouldn't have gotten anywhere near you if I had been. I'd have killed him first."

I know he would have. But he wasn't. And I'm glad for that. Mostly.

"Have they asked about it? The scar?" Manvir asks, glancing at it peeking from beneath the edge of my dupatta.

I don't want to talk about this. Don't want to see Manvir get worked up over it again. "I told them I fell."

"Hmm," Manvir says. "Simpler than the truth."

It is. It is simpler than explaining how I was standing in the shop when a bomb in the street exploded, shattering the large window in the storefront.

It is simpler than that half truth.

Simpler than saying that the glass didn't cut me until a man picked it up, pinned me against the wall, pressing my arms to my chest. Simpler than explaining that he held it to my cheek as I froze. Simpler not to repeat the words he uttered in Urdu, words whose meaning I still don't know, but whose shape and sound rattle inside my head when I'm sleeping, and then scream out like a peacock's shriek.

Simpler than saying that had the shopkeeper, Mr. Singh— who'd known me from the time Biji carried me into the shop to buy cakes and sweets when I was a baby and had greeted me that afternoon with a smile and a nod as I waited behind the others—had Mr. Singh not struck the man with the marble slab he used for pulling out naan . . .

Then I would have more scars than I have even now.

CHAPTER 7

MARGARET

"This is inexcusable," Mother complains, scowling at her wristwatch.

"Time is relative in the Punjab, Mother," I remind her. And it is. According to Daddy, no one seems to give much weight to appointment times or dates or anything like that. Here, people show up hours or even a day late to meetings or to repair the toilet or to install a telephone. Even our train from Delhi had sauntered into the station a full two hours behind and then idled there for another hour before we pulled away. And no one but Mother seemed to even notice.

"I told him precisely ten," she fumes.

"We could go without him," I offer, knowing full well she'll refuse. The pictures are the whole point for her.

Instead, she surprises me. "I suppose we must," she says, but she doesn't get into the car. She ducks back into the house. I'm left standing there with the driver, who shrugs and smiles apologetically.

Inside I hear Mother's voice echoing out from Daddy's study windows upstairs. I can't make out the words, but my father's soft murmured reply seems to calm her. Another minute ticks past, and just as I'm about to go in and see what's up, I hear her on the stairs, heels clicking double-time against the marble.

"We're ready," she announces, triumphant, sailing out the door, Tariq hurrying along behind her holding Father's Brownie camera like it's made of glass.

Tariq?

The driver straightens up, drops his smile, and steps forward as Tariq comes out. He chatters something at him in Punjabi, and I don't need to speak the language to understand that he's put out by Tariq being there. A lot of the staff are, as a rule. The housekeeper gives him the stink eye whenever he passes by. I've watched from my window when he comes back from his errands, when the guards on duty seem to take pleasure in moving as slowly as possible in opening the gate for him, glaring at him as he passes through.

I asked Father why Tariq is so unpopular. He told me he hadn't noticed, but expected it had to do with Tariq being Muslim.

"They're terribly suspicious of one another, particularly these days," Father said. I realized that all the men working here wore the turbans that the Sikhs were required to wear, hiding their long hair up inside. Even Anu's father and brother, when they came to fetch her for her afternoon off, wore the turban.

Only Tariq has his hair short, his head uncovered.

Tariq starts to reply to the driver, voice even, eyes low. He gets half a dozen words out before the driver begins shouting over him, and Mother intervenes.

"He's coming with us," she says firmly to the chauffeur, who looks like he wants to say more but instead forces a smile and an "of course, madam," before reaching to open her door.

I slide in beside her, feeling embarrassed for Tariq. Things get worse as he goes around to the other side of the car and climbs in the front seat. The driver huffs and fumes, but it isn't as if Tariq could ride in back with us. I suppose the driver wishes Tariq might ride along perched on the bumper or something. I see people do that all the time from my windows. There aren't many cars around, and those that do pass are often overflowing with passengers, some piled on the roof. The motorbikes are even worse. I once saw a single motorbike (no sidecar!) carrying a driver, his wife, and three children, one perched on the tank in front of the father, another on the handlebar, and the third, a baby, sleeping in his mother's arms while she balanced behind her husband.

At any rate, I'm glad Tariq gets to ride inside. Glad I can sneak looks at the back of his head.

The car roars to life and we're under way. Tariq hunches over the camera, fiddling with the knobs and dials.

"You do know how to use a camera, don't you, Tariq?" Mother asks him.

He nods. "Mr. Darnsley showed me how."

"Good," Mother says. "Then we've no need of the newspaperman. We can take our own photos and have them released back home. Always better to do things for oneself, right, Margaret?"

"Tariq can translate for us too," I add.

Mother jabs a finger at the air. "Quite so. You've really rescued us, young man," she says to Tariq, adding, "though my husband was loath to spare you."

Tariq murmurs his thanks and goes back to working with the camera.

I spend the rest of the ride alternating between staring at the back of his head and looking out the window. It's delicious to be out, wonderful to be seeing more of the city, even if it is from inside the car.

And even more perfect to be out with him. I sneak my looks at him, noticing how thick his hair his, how it curls a bit over his ears.

It takes us twenty minutes to break free of the constant stopping and starting as we inch through Jalandhar proper. At the outskirts, the road opens up a bit and the car picks up speed. We pass smaller marketplaces, the houses grow shabbier, the temples less frequent. And then, after ten miles of this, we begin to climb a squat hill.

At the top, the driver pulls to the side and gestures out the window, pointing. Tariq listens, then twists in his seat to speak to Mother and me.

"The camp is below," he explains. "The driver thought you would like to see it from here before he drives down into the valley."

I have to lean across Mother's lap to look, and what I find makes my mouth drop open.

I've never seen anything like it.

Tents and shanties lean up against one another, fighting for every spare square inch of space. Narrow lanes cut through the makeshift city like fissure cracks in a pane of glass. And everywhere are people. The whole camp, which stretches impossibly far, all the way to a muddy brown river in the distance, moves and thrums like an animal in too small a pen.

"Oh my," Mother whispers.

I say nothing, can't for how nervous I am all of a sudden. It's so much bigger than I expected. What can we possibly do? Suddenly I'm ashamed of that stupid camera in the front seat, ashamed of the fact that, though I wouldn't have admitted it before, I was a bit excited about the thought that snaps of me looking heroic might turn up in papers back home.

Even more shaming: I feel scared.

"Drive on," Mother whispers, and the driver steers us back onto the road, letting the long sloping track pull us down to the camp.

Two hours later I'm dressing the wounds on the gnarled feet of an old woman. She's impossibly thin and bent in all the wrong places, but she keeps smiling at me, beaming a grin that is no less beautiful for having only half its teeth. She chatters at me in Punjabi, pointing and smiling.

And though the sores are rancid, oozing wicked-looking yellow stuff, and I can't understand a word she's saying, I'm happy.

We were warmly welcomed by a couple of doctors and a man who is some kind of manager. They showed us around and told us about a few of the people here. They even arranged a few photos of us standing with some families, speaking to the administrator, handing out bars of soap, things like that. Tariq followed us meekly, snapping the pictures, but the doctors spoke fine English, so we had no need for a translator.

I thought Mother would have been as happy as a pig in mud, but after about half an hour she turned to the administrator and demanded that we be put to work. She even ordered Tariq to put down the camera and pitch in.

She told the doctors that I'd been a volunteer nurse during the war, and they set me up in their infirmary. The other physicians went off to another corner of the camp, another hospital where those with illnesses instead of injuries were being treated. But they left me here with some local women to work on the simple things, things that I could understand the trouble of from only looking. And I've been here since, dressing wounds, many of them festering, infected blisters like the ones this woman has.

They all got the sores the same way. Walking. Some hundreds of miles. This woman keeps pointing at her feet and then off to the northwest. "Rawalpindi," she says. "Far."

I know from Daddy's maps that it's nearly two hundred miles. It staggers me to think about her, a woman at least eighty, walking so far. That she would *have* to walk so far.

And Daddy even told me the whole thing was voluntary. No one—least of all the British—was making the Sikhs move into India and the Muslims move out to what would be Pakistan. Certainly the whole carving up of the Punjab had to do with creating separate states based on religion, but the "population exchange," as I heard Daddy call it, began because people on both sides were already starting to get territorial about their lands back when the boundaries themselves were just the whisper of an idea.

And now this. People without homes, without work, without food or prospects, crowding together in camps like this one on both sides. But it said a great deal about what they were running from if a place like this was better.

I finish up the woman's feet and realize how filthy and thirsty and hot I am. It's been hours since I've had a drop of water. I stand up, look around. I can see Mother and Tariq sitting next to some beds in another tent across the little alley. Mother's got her pencil and some paper out, listening as Tariq translates.

There is a pump off to the left in a bit of a clearing. I've heard it working away all morning, the metal arm groaning up and down, the water splashing in containers.

I take a step toward it and stumble—now that I don't have someone to look after, I feel suddenly exhausted. Half a dozen of the children playing around the pump see me at the edge of the tent and run over. They're so lovely-grubby, and their smiles are so bright. I let them touch my hair and giggle and chatter to one another when I arrived. I never thought I liked kids much, but I think I could spend all day with this lot if they let me.

The children surround me. I point at the pump and they shout, "Pani! Pani!"

I nod, repeat "Pani." They pull me over to the pump, laughing.

There is a long line of women and older children waiting at the pump, clay pots and jars resting on their hips. But as I approach, the ones near the front smile, grateful smiles, smiles to break my heart, but I suppose they're just glad to see someone who isn't here for the same reasons they are, someone who is here to help.

I smile back. My little friends go to work explaining that I'm thirsty. The women closest to the pump erupt into a sudden flurry of activity, one producing a dipper for me to sip from, another working at the handle with strength I wouldn't have guessed. But soon a cascade of water is splashing onto the mud. I step forward, let it spray my ankles, then crouch under and let it run over the back of my neck. The children clap and cheer. The women laugh. Mother might be mortified that I'll spend the rest of the day in a soaking blouse, but I don't care.

I move my head from under the flow, pick up the dipper, letting the water collect there. When I've gotten enough, I straighten and lift it in my hands. "Cheers," I call out to the ladies, who smile.

And just as I'm about to take my first sip, a hand reaches from behind, pulls my arm down hard, spilling the water from the dipper onto the earth.

I curse and spin around, but freeze when I see Tariq there, eyes wild. "Don't!" he says.

His hand is still locked around my wrist. I stare at it. One of the little children steps forward, arms crossed tight across his chest, staring daggers at Tariq. He growls something in Punjabi that Tariq ignores.

"The water," he says, and the doctor, the one from this morning, is rushing up behind him. He looks stricken at my wet hair and top.

"Did you drink any?" the doctor demands.

"I . . ." What is going on? "No," I manage.

He grabs my other wrist and pulls me away from the pump.

The children have gone still. They know something's up too. The chattering ladies fall silent behind us.

"What's wrong?" I ask. "Did I do something wrong?"

Mother crosses from the tent where she was working. "Margaret?" Her voice is all worry and warning.

"There is a problem," the doctor says. "I was coming to tell you—but saw your translator first," he nods at Tariq. "Good thing you moved so quickly, young man."

"Would someone please tell us what is going on?" Mother asks, looking from the doctor to Tariq and back again.

Tariq's hand is softer on my arm now, the vise loosening. He leans in and whispers, "There is cholera in the other infirmary tent. We must leave at once."

CHAPTER 8

TARIQ

"Oh, Lord," Mrs. Darnsley whispers.

"You're sure you didn't drink any of the water?" the doctor asks Margaret again. She shakes her head, eyes wide with fear.

"I think it might be best if you go for the time being," the doctor speaks in English to Mrs. Darnsley, but he cuts his eyes at me as if to say *get them out of here.*

"But what about all these people?" Margaret looks back at the line of women still waiting to collect water for washing, drinking, cooking.

"We don't know which supply is contaminated," the doctor says without much hope in his voice. "There are two pumps. It could be either one."

"Or both," Margaret says, her hand pressed against her chest.

Her blouse is damp from all the water she poured over herself. It clings to her skin and I can see . . .

Stop looking . . .

The doctor is talking again. "—will dig new latrines and issue warnings to boil all water," he says, but he sounds like he's already given up. I know enough about cholera to know why. Whole villages can be leveled by it. He turns to me, switches from English to Punjabi. He tells me to take the women home, that he will send word when it is safe for them to return.

"But if we don't drink any water, we'll be fine, won't we?" Margaret asks after I translate. "I'd like to stay."

No one's listening. They've all scattered, sending runners to spread the word. The doctor hurries over to the pump, announces that the water might be contaminated, that it must be boiled. Before he even finishes speaking, the women hurl questions at him about where will they find fuel to burn, what can they boil water in if they have no kettles, how long it will go on. There's nothing we can do.

"Follow me," I say to Mrs. Darnsley and Margaret, walking toward the tents where we had been working. I'd been helping Mrs. Darnsley record information about the people residing in the camp. I admit, I'm not sorry we got cut off. It was heartbreaking work. And sort of hopeless. I felt lower than a dog, sitting there as they told me their stories, all the while knowing that they knew I was Muslim. They'd all been pushed out by

Muslims so that other Muslims could come and take the homes and lands that had been theirs.

The same thing was happening here, only in reverse. My family would go to Pakistan when India became too dangerous for them. Would they end up in a camp like this one?

I prayed they wouldn't.

There wasn't much we could do, but we tried. While Margaret worked in the medical tent, Mrs. Darnsley and I were making two lists: one of the people living in the camp, and another of the people they'd lost during the migration. The people told us their stories, gave us their names, looking at me with fear while I translated for Mrs. Darnsley.

Everyone has lost someone. Lost as in dead and lost as in simply misplaced. One little girl clung to an old man—too old to even be her grandfather—while she told her story. Her parents were killed and she was separated from her two brothers near Rawalpindi. I never worked out her connection to the old man, but they held on to each other as if they were all they had left in the world. And then there was the woman, maybe a bit younger than my mother. Every time she opened her mouth and tried to speak, she'd fall apart, sobbing. We never got a word out of her.

They're just two of hundreds. Of thousands. In just one camp.

And with every terrible story, the image of that man I hit reared up in my mind again. Every time.

Still, I'd stay and listen all day if I thought it would do any good. If I thought—yes, I admit to this, too—that it would make up for what I did at the gurdwara. But the truth is, I think they were as uneasy with me there as I was being there. And I don't want to add to anyone's suffering or pain or fear, especially in a place like this.

They don't deserve it. Maybe I do, but they don't.

So I'm relieved for a real reason to get out of here. For their sakes. And mine.

I grab the camera from the tent—I think I only snapped half a dozen photographs. I hope Mrs. Darnsley won't take it badly.

"This way," I say to the ladies, cutting a path through the crowd. They still stop to stare at Margaret and her mother, who look as out of place here as I feel.

"Tariq!" Margaret calls nervously behind me. I'm moving too fast. I push my way through the crowd to collect them again. This time Margaret grabs my arm and holds on.

I lead them back to the edge of the camp, where the car waits by the road. A crowd still follows us, for no other reason than there is nothing else to do, nothing else to see.

Margaret keeps her hand clenched around my bicep. She holds on tight, squeezing, even though we're in view of the car, even though we're not going to get separated again.

And I'm a murkha, but I like her hand there. I can't help thinking, *There's a pretty girl on my arm.* A pretty English girl who needs me to protect her. I stand a little taller. It feels good.

But then I think of Darnsley. What would he say?

I expect his reaction would be a little like the driver's when he sees us coming up the rise toward the car. His mouth falls open and his face grows dark.

And even though I know it's gavara, I stare at him, dare him to say something. I slow down, let Margaret's arm sort of creep forward in mine until we're almost walking arm in arm, climbing up the hill. The driver is furious, and it feels good. Really good. Until Mrs. Darnsley reminds me how dangerous this is.

"Margaret, would you walk with me?" her voice breaks in suddenly, sharp edged. I feel Margaret's arm tense on mine briefly before she pulls away and goes back to lock arms with her mother, who helps her to the car.

Bewakoof! What did I just do? Of course she'd see. And now she might tell her husband. Hey, Allah . . .

I don't dare turn around. Maybe if I don't react, it will blow over. Maybe her mother will let it go. Maybe Margaret will let it go.

We reach the car. The driver opens the back door for the ladies, but before her mother can scoot over, like they did at the house, Margaret runs round to the passenger side, chasing after me as I move for my own door. We stand there a moment, alone, but not alone, and I wonder what I have gotten myself into. She is looking at me. *Looking.* At me.

This is bad. Bad, bad, bad, bad.

Mara.

There is nothing I can do but reach down and open the door for her. She gives me a faint little smile, one just for me, as she climbs into the backseat.

And in spite of everything, the heat rises in me. I close the door slowly.

She likes me. I've sort of known it from that first day. And it isn't like I haven't thought about her. About it. Her body . . . the way she looks sort of dangerous and exciting when I see her in the garden smoking one of her cigarettes. And she's English. I've thought about what it would be like to be with her. Or girls like her when I'm in England.

This is stupid. Murkha! She's even more off limits than Anupreet. She's Darnsley's daughter! His daughter! Everything hinges on impressing him, and I don't think sneaking around with his daughter—no matter how much she might want it— would do the trick of getting me to Oxford.

Unless . . .

Unless.

She could be helpful.

She is his daughter, after all. And a kind word from her on my behalf couldn't hurt.

Not that I'd do anything wrong. Just be her friend. Or maybe a little more. Just enough. It could work.

But I have to be careful. Very careful. A thing like this is like dynamite. Powerful. Unpredictable.

And dangerous.

CHAPTER 9

ANUPREET

I love Sunday afternoons. Every week, right after lunch, Mrs. Darnsley gives me my wages. Then Manvir comes to fetch me, and I spend the rest of the day at home, eating Biji's fine curry, and remembering what it was like to be with my family whenever I wanted.

But today Manvir did not come.

I waited at the gate for almost two hours, passing a few words with the guard stationed there as I wondered where my brother could be. After an hour I began to worry what might have happened to him, worry that a gang of boys—like the one that followed us in the market that first day—might have caught up with him. Worry that riots or violence in some other part of the city might have swept him up in its wake.

And then the worry passed to *knowing*. The only reason Manvir would not come was if he *could* not come.

But still I waited. Still I hoped. I had the small fold of rupee notes Mrs. Darnsley had just paid me in my little bag, ready to take home to Biji and Papaji. I thought to use some of it to hire a rickshaw. Papaji would be furious if I walked home, so maybe this once he wouldn't mind if I used some of the money to get a ride.

But what if Manvir turned up and found me gone? Part of me believed that as long as I waited in the shade of the sal tree, Manvir would come. If I found my own way home, it would be like giving up on him.

So I waited.

But then Mr. Darnsley must have noticed me standing there. He sent Margaret out to see what was the matter, and before I knew it, the driver had been summoned and I was leaving the gates of the yellow house in the backseat of the great black automobile.

I was riding in a car!

I've wondered a thousand times what it would be like. And now here I am.

But I feel awful for being so happy. Awful for letting my fear for Manvir get elbowed aside. But a car . . . carrying *me*.

It is almost too wonderful.

I've seen cars plenty. I've stepped out of the way of them when they come inching up a crowded margh. I've gazed at the faces inside, wondering what it would be like to be wrapped up in so much glass and metal, to have people scurry out of your way, to move without moving.

But being inside it is even better than I ever dreamed. The seat is warm and soft, like the bellies of the goats we kept when I was small. The car jerks and starts as the driver cuts a path through the street. The engine roars like a living thing, announcing it has somewhere to be, someone to carry there.

And I imagine for a moment that I am Margaret.

She's ridden in this car many times, and in probably dozens of others like it in London. I wonder if people stare at her there as they do here. Certainly not only because she's in the back of a motorcar. She looks as if she belongs in this seat, behind a driver, sealed up behind sparkling windows against a world, as if the car has its own air to breathe.

And now the people who look at her look at me. I'm not silly enough to think they're staring because my own black braid dazzles like her gold hair. They stare because I do not belong back here. I belong on the street with them, dodging the puddles and cattle and cart horses. They are wondering—I know they are—what I am doing in the backseat of a car, this car.

But I can pretend. I can pretend that this is what it feels like to be her. That this is how I'd feel all the time if someone drove me around. And the pretending takes me all the way home. The pretending helps me imagine I am someone else, keeps me from imagining what I will find at the end of this ride. Not a girl going to her house to see if it is still there. To see if her family is still there. To see . . .

The driver pulls up to the door, and I find it shut tight. Biji usually keeps it open during the day to let the air cool the house as it pulls through the front door and back through the cooking porch. But it is shut now. Shut tightly against whatever evil wind has kept my brother from coming to fetch me.

I spring out of the car, all the good feeling from the ride run dry as I try the latch. Locked.

"Papaji?" I call softly, drumming my fingers against the splintered surface of the door.

They take a long time to come. And when my father does finally call from the other side, I can hear the joy and worry in his voice. "Anu?"

"It's me," I say, hitching my dupatta around my shoulders and turning to wave the driver on. Margaret ordered that he wait to see me safely inside, but he seems anxious to get the car back.

I hear the sound of something heavy being moved, then the door opens. Papaji's eyes are red. He pulls me inside and into his arms. He murmurs a blessing, the words choked from his throat, and I begin to cry, so ashamed for having enjoyed my car ride so much.

"We tried to get a message to you," Papaji says, shutting the door, sliding the trunk back against it.

"What's going on?" I ask him, my eyes adjusting to the

darkened room. The windows are shuttered, the curtains drawn. Only the light from the kitchen and the cooking porch in the back of the house filter into the sitting room. Two women—I don't recognize either of them—move about in there, speaking softly, their Punjabi seasoned with the rougher accent that comes out of the north and west.

"Who are they?" I ask Papaji, wondering if we are hiding them for some reason.

He sighs. "Two of your biji's cousins. They turned up this week."

"From where?" I ask.

"The Kashmir," he replies. "Near Srinigar. They left with their husbands on foot. But they arrived here alone."

I don't have to ask what happened to the men. The women, my aunties, I suppose, look up from the doorway, study my face. They nod; one smiles a little. When they turn away, I hear them whisper something about my scar, one drawing a line across her cheek.

"They will stay?" I ask.

Papaji tells me they will, tells me they have no place else to go and that we will make the room, even with Uncle and his family arriving by train two weeks from now. It will be crowded, but we cannot let family go elsewhere. I haven't seen the camps, but I've heard about them and saw how rattled and quiet Margaret and her mother were when they returned from their outing to the one near Jalandhar this week.

"Where is Biji? Why didn't Manvir come for me?" I ask suddenly.

Papaji takes my hand, leads me to the door of my brother's room. Biji is there at his bedside, her back to me, leaning over my brother in his bed. At first I think he must be ill and worry that it might be something awful if it came on so quickly that no one had time to send word to me.

But then Biji shifts to the side, dips a cloth into a bowl of water waiting there, and the water that runs from her hands as she squeezes out the rag is a rusty red-brown.

And then I see my brother's face.

If he were not in his own bed, with my own mother bending over him, whispering prayers, I would not know him.

One eye is so swollen that the skin stretches tight across it, the slit in the middle swallowing up his eyelashes. The other is half-open, but it too is crusted with blood. The skin around his left ear is torn, ripped ragged and still seeping. He will need stitches, and I wonder if Papaji will be able to do them himself. Manvir's arm lies awkwardly across his chest, his wrist bulging with what looks like a nasty break.

I rush to Biji, who hugs me quickly. I study Manvir over her shoulder. How can it be him?

"What happened?" I whisper. I can't stop the tears. Can't stop watching his chest rise and fall just to make sure he is alive. Not Manvir, not my brother. . . .

"His friends brought him home to us this way." Papaji's voice is edged with something hard. Anger, maybe? Biji still doesn't speak.

"His friends did this to him?" I ask with shock.

"Nahi," Papaji says.

Biji speaks for the first time. "They might as well have," she says bitterly. "Leading him off to trouble that way."

I stiffen, look at Papaji, whose eyes are stone.

"Manvir made his choice," he says, and I know what he means.

Oh, Manvir. None of his friends, not Balwinder or Mahinder or Navdeep or any of the rest did anything without it being Manvir's idea first. It had always been that way. And only Biji could not see it.

He'd been so angry the last few times he walked me home. Worse even than that day we were followed. I shouldn't be surprised that he did something stupid. Something dangerous.

"Tell me," I demand as I wipe away a tear and move around to the other side of the bed.

Papaji crosses his arms. "We do not know how it started. But they were near the old mosque, the one with the school nearby—"

He pauses. I lower myself onto the bed, take up Manvir's uninjured hand.

"They were boys brawling," Biji says defensively, "and got carried away."

But I know she is making excuses. If it was near the mosque, if the others were Muslim, it couldn't have been an accident. Try as I might, I can't think of any reason Manvir and his friends might have for going to that neighborhood.

No reason other than doing something terrible.

Papaji's voice is quiet. "Balwinder said there were three of them on your brother at once. But they all managed to get away somehow."

I can hear the doubt in his voice. Papaji doesn't think Manvir's friends told him the whole truth. But looking at Manvir, it doesn't seem likely he'll be telling any of us anything soon.

Stupid, Manvir! Stupid men with their stupid fighting! I'm so angry with him. So angry that he let this happen to himself. That he wanted it to happen!

But then I remember that he wasn't so angry before I got cut.

My eyes burn as I realize this. It wasn't my fault I was attacked. Maybe Manvir's trouble wasn't his fault either. He could have just been walking by and gotten drawn into a riot.

I want it to be true. But somehow I know it's not.

No. He wanted this. He'd wanted to track down the man who attacked me. He wanted to fight those boys that day we were chased through the market. I remember what he said: *Sick of running. Sick of it.*

And now I feel sick that maybe he did this because of what happened to me.

At least he's alive. Thank God he's alive. "Has he been awake?"

"Some," Papaji says. "We've sent for the doctor." I take the rag from Biji's hand as she rises to fetch a bowl of clean water. I dab it across my brother's brow. He looks so different to me now, and not only because of his injuries. I *see* him differently too. See the same disease in him that seized that young man in the shop that day, the one who cut my face. *How different can they be?* I wonder.

No. No. Manvir would never do anything like that.

"He will be all right, Anu," Papaji says, placing a hand on my head.

All right so long as they can keep him indoors. As long as he can't get out of bed, he will be. Because he can't fight and brawl and let his anger lead him if he can't walk, can he?

So I pray. A silent prayer that my brother's wounds will take a long, long time to heal.

CHAPTER 10

MARGARET

Damned cholera.

We haven't been back to the camp since that first time. Mother got word that the outbreak had spread and then, just as they seemed to be getting things in hand, the hospital tents were raided, some of the residents there beaten up even worse than when they came in, and all the supplies stolen.

I take another drag on the cigarette, try to make it last, know I'll be out by the weekend if I keep up at this pace. Inside I hear Mother on the telephone again, trying her hardest to find some other way to make us useful, some other way to get the pictures of us looking righteous to send back to London. The other photographer she hired never did turn up, and we haven't printed the snaps Tariq took that day. Mother reckons he couldn't have gotten near enough to secure any keepers. I hope it means we get to try again. Not because of the pictures themselves. And not just because it might mean another morning out with Tariq.

I want to do something to help. Truly. Anything would be better than wasting my days, burning through my cigarettes too quickly. Even the garden and my hiding spot out here seem too small now. I'm not doing any good around here. I've tried to help Daddy, but I'm mostly in the way. And I've written half a dozen letters every day, some to the girls at school or my grandmother or anybody else I can think of. But even that gets tired, what with not having anything new to write about.

I want to do something.

I haven't been able to forget how kindly the people looked at me as I dressed their wounds, or how good it felt to be helping. I expect that's a bit vain, but I can't help it. And I can't forget the children. So many of them. Not just in the camps, but everywhere. Every time I've been anyplace in the car and the driver has to stop and wait for the road to clear, their little hands tap on the windows, begging.

And it dawns on me—how could I have been so thick?—that we don't have to go so far as the camp or even out into the city to find people in need. I drop the cigarette—it's close enough to singe my fingers now, anyway—into the dirt, grind it out with my toe, and kick it into the weeds.

I cross around to the back of the house, the little door that leads to the alley. From the back windows, I've seen the staff hauling the rubbish out here. And I've seen the people who come and pick through what we throw out. I've watched them—old women, younger men, all manner of folk, but mostly children. And one boy—shoeless and barelegged, his long green shirt-thing falling almost to his knees—is there every day, sometimes more than once a day, pawing through the garbage for treasure.

I told Father about him, asked him if we couldn't do something for the boy, maybe ask one of the household staff to talk to him on our behalf. But Father said no, said we mustn't get involved with disrupting the way of life here, and that our help could actually hurt him in the long run. When I said that didn't make sense, Mother said what if we did help him, what would happen to him after we left? And then I said maybe you could take a picture of me giving him some shoes and then she snapped her cap at me and sent me to my room.

So that was that. But he's still there, every day, and he's caught on to me watching him now, looking up to wave when he arrives at the heap with his cotton sack thrown over his shoulder.

I could do something, I think. For him. All I'd have to do is open that door.

But I saw him already today, early in the morning. He won't be back. So I wander inside, take my time on the stairs, and make my way back to my room. At home, when Mother confined me, I always had my piano. I could play like a dream even before the whole Alec debacle, but I improved loads when I was shut up in the house after everything went to sixes and sevens. Mother was terrified I'd fall in love with another GI given half a minute out of doors, so she didn't even bat an eye when I moved on from Mozart and Debussy to teaching myself Cole Porter tunes from the radio. So long as I stayed in the house. So long as she knew where I was, I guess.

But without the piano, I'm bored. *Bored.* I'd love to pop out and explore a bit of Jalandhar. I think I would, at least. It's a bit overwhelming, even just watching from my window. All the people constantly moving, the noises, the voices ringing out in words that are meaningless to my ears.

Mother and Daddy would never let me go out alone, but they're too busy to run me about. Mother keeps putting me off, saying not until Daddy has a moment to escort us. But he's either rushing out to meetings at Governor Jenkins's house or cloistered in his study room, the tables spilling coiled maps like brittle bolts of linen towering on the racks at Bennison's back in London. Which makes me wonder if there's even a decent dressmaker's anywhere in this city, someplace I can get something to wear that won't make me feel like I'm roasting alive.

Because God in heaven, I am. And there's precious little relief from it. Even at night I sweat through my sheets. The only respite we get are short, heavy downpours. It cat-and-dogs it for a good hour or two, every other day or so, but when it stops, it's even hotter and steamier and stickier than before. Father says all the locals are worried at how late the monsoon proper is in arriving this year, and I for one wish it would bloody hurry up and come.

I ooze across the hallway to Father's study, sure if I were barefoot I'd be leaving wet footprints behind me on the tile. My dress sticks to my back.

"All right, Daddy?" I ask, leaning over to kiss the top of his head as he sits at his desk. It is cooler in here, kept shadier by the veranda roof so the study never gets the direct sunlight. Though it still swelters like hell in July, there is a bit of a breeze owing to the extra sets of windows. And Daddy has a small brass fan set up by his feet—he can't have it any higher where it might blow all his precious maps about. He's promised to find me one, but I'm not holding my breath.

Besides, it gives me something to do, coming down the hall to have the fan blow the breeze up my knickers. He doesn't even take particular notice of me when I wander in here and look over his shoulder at the map spread wide on the table.

"How many maps of the Punjab can there be?" I ask, lifting up the end of one of the stacks.

Father straightens, stands, stretches, and finally looks at me. "They're all different. Maps showing historical boundaries between villages, before the Raj. Maps showing water and mineral resource deposits. Maps showing sacred sites. Did you know that half the holy places in the Punjab are claimed at once by Hindus, Muslims, and Sikhs?"

I shake my head.

"Damned tangle, if you ask me. Mountbatten's asked the impossible—that August fifteenth deadline. Just over a month left to divide a country thousands of years old. Four or five weeks to finish sorting out thousands of years of shared mythology, geography . . ."

He shakes his head.

I still say nothing, but move closer to study the map on the table. I hadn't considered carving up the subcontinent might be so difficult.

"Why don't you do what Mother used to make Cousin Lucy and me do when we had a sweet to share? Have one of us cut and the other choose which half they want?"

Father snorts; his shoulders give one short convulsion of laughter. "A fine idea. But such an arrangement relies on the concerned parties gathering in the same space together without devolving into a pack of screaming monkeys."

I nod. He forgets that Lucy and I could outdo howling monkeys any day.

"And it would take away the one tiny thread of unity these people seem to share. A hatred for the crown. And a mutual desire to have us to blame for the outcome when both Pakistan and India feel shorted by the boundaries. If they don't have us to rail against, even when we're gone, they'll go at each other even more viciously than they already are. Mountbatten may not understand much, but he knows that. Knows how important it is to give them another target for their rage—"

"But the people love him, don't they?"

Father shrugs. "Well enough. He's the face of the British secession from the Jewel of the Empire. How could they not?"

He's right, I suppose. Even I managed some affection for the most horrid teachers back at boarding school when term was up. Sometimes the gladness that you soon wouldn't have to see a person again got twisted into a kindness before you were even rid of them.

"At any rate," Father says, returning to his chair and the set of pencils he's been using to mark this map, "we're as responsible as anyone for making these people hate each other. When it served the crown to divide them, to favor one group over another, we did it shamelessly. Only fair that we do our bit to clean up the mess, and look defeated in the bargain. Least we can do."

Tariq appears, hovering in the doorway. The breeze from the open window seems to blow warmer through the room. He somehow seems shyer now about looking at me, even after he was so gallant in the camp. But I think I see him glancing my way at times. Though maybe that's only on account of how much I find myself staring at him.

"Sir?" he says softly. Father looks up, eyes lighting on the note in Tariq's hand.

"Bring it here, please," he says, beckoning him forward.

Tariq gives a quick nod, crosses round to the other side of the desk, and hands the note over. Father breaks the wax seal with his thumb and unfolds the paper. The letterhead bears the stamp of the governor general.

I study him while my father reads. Tariq really is good-looking, I have decided. Shoulders nearly as broad as Alec's were, and skin like perfectly browned toast. He is not sweating, not like Daddy and me, and I suppose that makes him even more attractive. He stands there, watching my father read, waiting for him to say something, hands folded behind him, the long white shirt I've learned they call a kurta skimming the tops of his thighs, his pants—something like the riding jodhpurs folk wear back home—loose above the knee but tapering to a snug fit around his calves.

"Ah," Father says.

"What is it?" I ask.

He holds up a finger, reads for another moment, then says, "They're extending the reach of the survey trip Tariq and I are to make next week. We'll be gone a few extra days."

"Can I come?" The words fly out of my mouth before I can stop them.

He shakes his head. "Afraid not, pet. All business, and hours in the car. They're intent on me getting all the way up to Himachal Pradesh in the north. Radcliffe needs some current surveys of the area."

"Why doesn't the tosser go himself?" I grumble.

"Don't say 'tosser,'" Father snorts, but he doesn't mean it like Mother does. "Anyway, Radcliffe's too much of a lightning rod. He'll stay sequestered in Delhi. His is the final say, and his will be the name history signs across this canvas," he says, nodding at the map.

"Is that fair?"

Father mops the back of his neck with his handkerchief. "This isn't necessarily the kind of work that you want history remembering you for," he says quietly.

"But Mother thinks—"

"I know what your mother thinks," he says in a clipped sort of a voice, in a way that makes it clear he believes she's wrong.

"Did you know Michelangelo didn't do all the painting on the Sistine Chapel?" he asks suddenly. "That the design was his, but he had apprentices who completed portions of the frescoes? Their names are lost, but their work is still there for everyone to see."

I'm only half listening as I glance at Tariq, trying to make him look at me. He's just standing there like butter won't melt in his perfect mouth, as if he's not hearing a word we're saying. But I know his English is good even if his accent makes everything sound all queer.

"Maybe this is a bit like that," Daddy says, his voice going soft, like he wishes it were true.

After a beat, Tariq clears his throat.

"Sorry, Tariq, nearly forgot you were there." Father leans forward, scrawls a reply confirming that he'll amend his itinerary. Tariq takes it, then slips it into the pocket at his breast. He clears his throat again.

"Sir?"

"Hmm?" Father looks up.

"With your permission, may I stop in to visit with my family for luncheon after sending the telegram?"

He speaks slower, with more care than when we first came. I wonder if I make him nervous. I sort of hope so. It would mean he thinks about me. Is aware of me. But then he's guarded and careful with everyone, not just me.

Father nods his assent. "Don't take too long, though. I've need of you this afternoon."

"Certainly, sir," Tariq says, a grin breaking across his face. For an instant I get a glimpse of him—the real him—smiling, happy, unguarded. And he's even better looking for it. Really, with a smile that deadly, I'm relieved he's so bloody serious all the time. "Thank you, sir." He bows quickly, and when he lifts his eyes again, they fall on me, and the smile falters a tic. He looks away, suddenly shy again.

Well, then.

Tariq bolts out the door. I watch him leave, longing to go with him, and not just because I'm desperate to get out of this house.

I sigh and turn so the fan can cool the backs of my knees, and rest my bum against the desk.

"Can I go out too, Father?"

"What for, Meggie?" he asks, reaching for his fountain pen.

"A bit of a shop, I think," I say. "I wonder if they might have some clothes ready-made that might be more suitable to this heat."

He inspects the nib of the fountain pen, looks up at me. "Not by yourself, of course."

I shake my head. "Mother might come," I offer. "Anupreet would, certainly."

He takes a deep breath and sighs. "I'm sure we can just send out for what you might—"

"Please, Father, let me go. Only for an hour. Nothing will happen. And we'll just pop into the market across the way. Close enough that even the guard from the front gate could come with us if you wanted."

He pulls a clean sheet of paper onto the blotter. "One hour. Be back in time for lunch."

I pop to my feet and bend over to kiss him on the cheek. "Thanks ever, Daddy!"

He pulls open his desk drawer and fishes his billfold from the mess. "I've no idea how much you'll require," he says, counting out the notes into my hand. He gives me four hundred rupee in soft, rumpled notes.

I kiss him again and run out the door to find Anu before he can change his mind.

Anu looks stunned when I tell her that Father is sending us out shopping. At first I think she simply doesn't understand me, the way they shake their heads here to mean both yes and no, the confused look in her eye. But then I show her the money, point at the market stalls out across the lane from my window, her eyes growing wide like she's afraid, but that doesn't make sense. I reach for the pink tunic she's wearing over her matching pink pants.

"I need something to wear that won't make me feel like a boiled potato," I say.

"Ah," she says back, but I'm still not sure she understands.

I roll my eyes and pull her by the hand with me down the stairs and out the front door.

The porter sees us coming and stands taller, thrusting out his chest. The salute, I suspect, is only partly out of respect for my position as the daughter of his employer. I've noticed men have a hard time not reacting when Anu appears.

"We're going to the market," I tell him.

He cocks his head sideways but doesn't reach for the latch that holds the gate shut.

I point at the stalls in the distance again, "Shopping?" *Damn this language.*

He smiles apologetically, showing off a gleaming gold tooth. I throw up my hands, turn to Anu. "Tell him, would you?"

Anu nods once but doesn't speak at first. She looks back to the house, as if expecting someone to run out and fetch us back inside. Then she looks at me. "Go on," I say, smiling. "It's all right." I know she understands English better than she speaks it, but I don't understand why she's hesitating.

She smiles back shakily and then faces the guard, speaking in a stream of Punjabi so rapid and lovely it's like one of Schubert's arpeggios.

The porter's smile falters; he looks back and forth between our faces and behind us to the house, as if he too is looking for someone to tell him that this is all some kind of mistake. But after a second more he unlatches the gate and lets us pass into the street.

He calls out something to Anu.

"Haan ji," she says back, without turning round.

"What did he say?" I ask.

She gathers up her words, thinking them out before speaking them.

"This market only," she says.

I nod. This market will be plenty. I'm almost skipping as we cover the half a block between our front gate and the spot where the market begins. The outermost stalls face the street, selling such an assortment of items that Harrods might claw off and bury itself out of shame.

Each stall displays its wares proudly. We pass by one holding thousands of odd little slippers, another with pyramids of fruits I've never seen, another with towering stacks of brightly colored fabric. There is a paper seller, something like a drugstore, a jeweler, a bookshop, a toy shop, a spice merchant, and one selling cooking tools. And it goes on and on, more of the same goods mixed in with unexpected ones here and there, each turn revealing more makeshift lanes and corridors between the merchants.

I am so busy gaping and grinning that I don't realize how tightly Anu is squeezing my hand.

I look down at it, see her knuckles showing white where she's woven her fingers into mine. "Anu?" I ask.

She cuts her eyes away from the long alley of shops ahead of us and looks at me. She forces a smile, but she doesn't seem herself.

"Anu, what's the matter?" The girl has been acting funny all week. But she won't tell me why, and she won't explain why her family didn't show up to collect her on Sunday.

She tries to shake me off, pulls me inside the market proper, but something is the matter. I plant my feet, make her stop walking.

"Anu, are you all right?"

She takes a breath. "Yes, miss. Sorry, miss."

"Don't bloody apologize—"

"You want salwar-kameez, miss?" she interrupts, gesturing at her outfit.

I sigh. "I suppose so," I say, giving up on figuring out her trouble for now. "But where do we start?" From where I stand, I can see three different shops selling clothing. I cast about looking for something to distinguish one from another, but my eye lands on a pile of brown bumpy things tumbled in a bin in front of a grocer's. "What is this?" I ask, lifting one up.

"Imli," Anu replies, though she barely glances at it. I lift it to my nose to sniff the rough hull, but get no sense of what might be inside. The shopkeeper has been watching us, and he reaches for one and splits it along some invisible seam. It falls open like a peapod, revealing fruit the size of small apples inside. He pulls one out and hands it to me, grinning. I sniff it, look at Anu, who is still scanning the market stalls. I nibble a bit off the fleshiest side and my mouth immediately contracts in spasms. The flavor is at once sour and sweet. Almost smoky. The grocer laughs; Anu turns and looks horrified at what I'm eating.

"Nahi!" She frowns, casting her eye at the shopkeeper. She scolds him in Punjabi before slipping back to her halting English. "For cooking—pastes," she explains. Her eyes light up as she reaches past me and pulls out another fruit, a scaly-looking thing that fits nicely in her palm, the pinkish-orange color a match for her tunic.

"Lychee," she explains. "For eating."

The grocer hands her a knife, which she uses to expertly pull back the leathery hide. Inside lies flesh so white and pure and gleaming that it's like a giant pearl. She cuts off a sliver and hands it to me. The fruit is slippery in my hand, so I pop it into my mouth before I drop it. And the flavor is wonderful. Sweeter than strawberries, but similar. And the aroma of it is even stronger than the flavor, like a perfume, almost, as it lingers in the air, enhancing the taste.

I close my eyes and sigh with bliss. Anu laughs and helps

herself to a slice. She negotiates a price with the vendor as I grab the lychee from her hand, take a bite straight from it in a way that would make Mother cringe. I give Anu the smallest of the notes Father gave me. She collects back several coins and we go on our way, nibbling at the fruit, the sweet sticky juices running down my wrist.

By the time we settle on a clothing shop to try, I have to resort to wiping my hands on my skirt. But even then the fragrant stickiness lingers as we sit on cushions inside the shop and two men and a woman parade different outfits before us.

There are so many of them, and I'm so dazzled by the colors and the variety that I haven't even begun to think about choosing.

"Miss?" Anu asks gently as the pile of options grows past my knees. "Your father wants you back?"

"By lunch." I nod. If I'm late returning this time, he likely won't let me out again at all.

"Show me that blue," I say, pointing at one near the top of the stack. The clerk pulls out a blue salwar-kameez like the set Anu wears, the shade a bit more subdued but still a lovely turquoise. At the neckline a yoke of embroidery in gold and silver thread forms a collar of sorts, the pattern repeated on the cuffs at the three-quarter sleeves and near the ankles of the trousers.

"Does it come in my size?" I ask Anu. I'm considered tall at home, but I feel even more a freak here in India.

She looks confused for a moment, then her eyes light up.

"They sew," she says, pantomiming stitching a seam with her hands. "To fit you."

I nod, wondering how long that might take, but pick out another set in the same lightweight fabric, this time in a pearly green. This set has beading instead of the embroidery.

My decisions give the shopkeeper confidence, and his wife, for surely she is his wife, goes to another shelf and pulls out a fold of purple silk. She unfurls it, letting it cascade across the other piles of clothing like a wave breaking on the shore. I can't help but reach out and touch it, sticky fingers be damned. The silk is so luxuriant and light, the pattern of fine silver and darker purple woven into it in swirls and paisleys, all changing with each shift of the fabric like it really is the surface of some deep, wonderful sea. Marvelous.

"It's just fabric, though," I point out to Anu.

She smiles. "Sari," she explains. "No sewing. Here." She pulls me to my feet and she and the woman together fold and tuck the fabric around my body, starting at my waist to create a floor-skimming skirt, the pleats so sharp and perfect as they fold that I can scarcely believe this is the same long run of fabric. Then they twist and tuck the rest of the silk up and over my body.

"Sari." Anu beams.

I look at myself in the small glass at the rear of the shop.

"I'll take it," I say.

Anu looks surprised but doesn't argue, chattering with the

shopkeeper, who looks delighted. She pulls the sari off my body, revealing me in my plain, sad, sweaty dress, and then produces a string that she uses to measure my waist, bust, hips, upper arms, and inseam of my legs, calling out the numbers to the younger of the men. I'm a little mortified to have my measurements broadcast this way, but no one else seems to notice.

"They make blouse and petticoat for under sari," Anu says, "and alter salwar-kameez. Then send to the house."

"Should I pay them now?" I ask.

She looks at them. "Kitna hai?"

They call out a number.

Anu makes a face, shakes her head sadly. Then she calls back another number.

The wife looks at her husband, nods once.

"Two hundred rupee . . . all three," Anu says.

I reach for the fold of money and count it out into the man's palm. Anu gives them our address, though they probably have a decent notion of where the only blond girl in all of Jalandhar is living at the moment, and we are on our way.

"Hurry," she says.

I follow her toward the edge of the market where we entered, but that sound—the same instrument I heard that day we arrived in the car—catches my ear again. I stop, grab her arm. "Do you hear that?"

She looks at me, concerned.

"The music?" I beg.

She gives that nod/non-nod of her head that tells me nothing. "This way," I say, following the sound deeper into the market.

The music grows louder as we barrel past the stalls and slip between the shoppers. They all stare as we rush by, but this time I don't care. I only care about finding the source of that music. Finally we are in a darkened corner of the market, far from the more necessary items of food and clothing and cooking pots.

An old man who looks like he's been carved out of wood sits in a stall playing a small sort of piano. It rests on the floor in front him, the keyboard about half the length of my piano at home. And instead of pedals, there are knobs and pulls along the front below the keys. At the back of the thing a bellows is attached, folding in and out as he plays.

It bleats, sort of, or whines, I don't know which. The bloody thing is like the product of some tryst between a church organ and a set of bagpipes, what with all the stops and things. It's amazing, really, like a cat with wings. It shouldn't be so pretty, but it is. And the tone . . . the tone of the thing is hypnotic, one note or chord yielding to the next one, no one waiting its turn to be heard. It makes me almost laugh to hear it, to imagine the sheet music for it, all the notes crowding up against each other, like the way people here won't queue up for love or money.

The old man's eyes are shut, his lips moving as he plays, the sound droning on in the nicest possible way as his right hand drifts up and down the short keyboard, the left patiently working at the bellows, pumping steady breath into the thing as if it'll die if he stops. And I instantly know I have to have one.

I look up to see the other instruments arranged in the shop—drums and a couple of those long-necked guitar jobs I've seen before. There are a few more of the pianos there as well, one lacquered in a shiny red with pearly elephants inlaid on the sides.

"What is that?" I ask Anupreet.

"Harmonium," she says, smiling, shoulders moving slightly, as if the music makes her want to dance.

"Kitna hai?" I point at the red one, repeat the phrase Anu has used every time she's needed to ask the price of something. The shopkeeper stops playing, says something in Punjabi.

Anu's mouth falls open.

"Well?" I ask.

"Three hundred rupee," she whispers.

"Tell him we'll pay him when he delivers," I say.

Anu's eyes widen. She knows Father hasn't approved the purchase of a harmonium, but I know he'll understand.

The man bows his head as Anu translates, pointing in the direction of the compound. He says something back, and she turns to me. "It will arrive this afternoon."

I smile, clap my hands together, already eager for the feel of those keys beneath my fingers.

We hurry back through the market and are almost across the street when a small cluster of children appear in front of us.

They hold their empty hands up to us and gesture feeding themselves from those barren palms.

Their message couldn't be clearer.

I think with guilt about the fruit I've just eaten in the market, about the lunch I'll tuck into soon. About the hundreds and hundreds of rupees I've just spent.

Anu speaks to the children, waving them off, but is unable to muster any real annoyance for them. He is among them—the little boy in the green shirt. I reach into my pocket. I've still got money left. I wonder if it is enough—

Anu's hand clamps down tighter on mine. I look up and find her shaking her head, warningly.

I let her drag me through the throng and back inside the gate. The porter begins shouting at the children in earnest, his voice blaring and barking like a guard dog. The beggars scatter, giggling, bare feet carrying them in all directions.

"So sorry, miss," Anu says to me as we reach the front door.

I shake my hand free of hers, cross my arms. "What harm can it do to give them something?" I demand.

Anu looks for all the world like she doesn't have enough words to explain this to me. "It is not the way," she says finally.

I don't want to have the same argument with her that I've been having with my parents. "Bugger all," I say churlishly. Anu looks pained, though I'm dead sure she doesn't know what "bugger" means. How I wish she did. She's the nearest thing I've got to a friend here. Shopping with her was such fun, so easy, that it felt almost normal, that I hate to end it this way. Hate that she doesn't understand me, hate that I don't know if I'll be here long enough to understand the rules, to know why it's so bloody awful of me to give a few pennies to some children. And I hate that when I say "bugger," she doesn't know enough to be shocked or amused, hate that she thinks my pique has to do with her. But maybe it does. She's convenient for it, after all. I'm a bit muddy about it myself, but it strikes me that I can like her so much one second, be so glad for her company, but the next I'm annoyed with her for not understanding me, or jealous of her for being so gorgeous.

Why must I be so awful?

Old Shibani appears in the door and calls to Anu to come in and serve the luncheon.

"I don't mean to take it out on you," I manage, reaching for her arm.

Anu's eyes soften. "All fine," she says. And like that we're friends again, I guess.

She goes into the house, back to her work, and I'm alone, the rupee coins and notes heavy in my pocket, where they do no one any good.

CHAPTER 11

TARIQ

Ammi keeps stacks of steaming parathas coming and I devour them, scooping up the rogan josh, barely stopping to chew the chunks of lamb. I feel like I haven't eaten in days, and I'm supposed to be back at the Darnsleys' soon, but even if I weren't in such a hurry, I don't think I could slow down.

I had no idea how much I could miss Ammi's cooking. The old Hindu woman who cooks at the Darnsleys' is awful. She barely uses any meat, and when she does, it's only chicken and it comes out all dry and stringy. Plus, she's stingy with the portions she sets aside for me. I asked for seconds one time (even though the first helping wasn't all that good). She ignored me and took the plate away.

Ammi's curry is so good, and I can have as much as I want. The heat and flavor and oil almost make me forget work, forget

Oxford, forget the way I can't stop staring at Anu, forget the way Margaret won't stop staring at me. I just eat.

"You are growing thin," Ammi clucks. "Too much of this riding all over town on the bicycle for that man, too little good food to go with it."

I grab another paratha, rip it in half, and wipe up what remains of the curry in my dish before I stuff it into my mouth.

"Has Abbu come home for lunch yet?" I ask.

Ammi shakes her head. "He and Arish pack tiffins to eat at the shop now. They stay busy these days as people prepare to move." Muslim families with the wealth to move have been coming to Abbu to convert their money into gold and gems. Soon he'll do the same with our savings.

I reach for the pitcher of milk and pour myself a glass. Even the milk is richer, somehow sweeter here than what I get at the Darnsleys' house. Is this what it will be like when I go to England? No one there will make rogan josh like Ammi's, no one will worry if I only eat half a dozen parathas. For the first time I have a strange thought: *Will it be worth it?*

Before, I thought about only one half of life in Oxford. Me in classes or the libraries or a pub talking about important things. But now, as the possibility becomes something more real, I've thought about the other half. How alone I'll be. There will be no one who knows me. For the first time I've started to realize what it will mean to miss my family. There will be no one to feed me, no one to be with in the evening, no one to kneel next to during evening prayers, no home near enough to visit.

The knowing of it gapes wide inside me, hungrier than my empty belly did when I walked in the door.

I throw back the rest of the milk and pop to my feet.

But it will be worth it. When I come back, it will all be worth it.

"Shukriya, Ammi," I say, leaning down and kissing the top of her head quickly. She reaches over her shoulder and grabs my hand, pats it once, and lets me go. I collect my bike at the gate and head off.

There is a parade on the main road. Something for one of the Hindu festivals. It'll take longer to get back with the traffic, but I don't care much. Darnsley won't notice. He takes a long time to eat, and I should make it back before he finishes the pipe he smokes before going back up to his office to work.

So I ride slowly, my belly heavy with Ammi's cooking, wondering about what else I will miss when I go.

I've heard England is quiet. People call it peaceful, but I can't imagine it. I wonder what it will be like to live without the noises of home.

The sound of the vegetable wallah with his cart, hawking what he's got for sale as he wheels up the row of houses.

Or the dohl beating out its rhythm a block over as the worshippers march in their parade.

A pack of dogs barking in the distance.

Another sound yanks me out of my trance as a horn blares, pulling me back to the crowded street.

I look up and stop the bicycle in time to avoid the rickshaw that nearly cuts me down. I wait for a gap in the flow of traffic and look across to the small market square.

The shops here are mostly run by Hindus and Sikhs, though the market itself sits at the crossing between a gurdwara and the mosque my family attends. For the moment, at least, everything is as it should be. The brass pots still hang from the rafters of the stalls, the piles of spices are undisturbed, the beaded jutis wait in neat rows.

Everything is in place except for the figure I see arguing with the keeper of the shoe stall.

Sameer.

I narrow my eyes as I wonder what business he has here. The jutis are mainly bridal shoes or fancy ones.

The shopkeeper looks mad. He jabs a finger at Sameer's face. Sameer tilts his head to one side. But then the shopkeeper thrusts a fat wad of rupee notes into Sameer's hand, takes a short, deep breath, chest rising and falling as he crosses his arms. Sameer gives a bit of a bow, and as he turns to go, I see he is grinning and scanning the street to see if anyone is watching.

The crowd around me begins to move as they make their way across the lane, but I stay rooted to the spot. And I don't move until I see Sameer slip into a goldsmith's shop a few doors away from the one he just left.

I know I should be going back. But I have to know what he's up to.

I stow the bike next to a few others leaning against a brick wall and duck inside a bookseller's stall. I hang back in the shadows and watch across the market as Sameer collects another wad of rupee notes from another shopkeeper. It only takes a moment this time before he walks slowly to the corner and then sprints away.

"Devil," a voice says behind me.

I jump, turn, and find the bookseller leaning over his counter. At first I think he means me, but then he jabs at the window where I just watched Sameer run away.

"That one is an ibalisa," he repeats.

Then he looks at me.

I have no turban on my head to match his.

He lifts his chin, squares his jaw.

I am a Muslim. He is a Sikh. He must think I have come to make trouble.

Like Sameer.

I panic. Part of me wants to run, but the other part wants to show him that I am not like Sameer. My eyes scan the books arranged in the window. I pick up the smallest one, the cheapest-looking one, and flip through the pages. It smells old. The book is in English, which isn't surprising: probably half the books in the shop are. But I don't care what it says, only what the price is. I don't even notice the title or anything else about the book before I decide I can afford the few rupees. I hand the book to the merchant; one of his eyebrows shoots up, but he takes my money and hands the book back to me.

"Shukriya," I say as I stumble back onto the street, feeling his eyes burning on the back of my head. I toss the book in the basket of the bike and notice the title.

Men and Women: Poems by Robert Browning.

Chutiyaa. I should have looked closer at the text. I might have at least gotten something useful instead of a biratha book of poetry.

I stroke down on the pedal, weave my way across the street, wondering what Sameer is playing at now, blaming him for the way I just wasted my money. He has a talent for driving me into trouble, even when he has no idea that he's doing it.

Twenty minutes later I'm within view of Darnsley's compound when I see Margaret and Anupreet leaving the market across the lane. I stop the bicycle and dismount. They are an odd pair, Margaret so tall, shoulders rounded forward, skin ghostly white, her yellow hair almost the same color as the walls. Next to her Anupreet, skin gleaming like a rare brown moonstone in one of Abbu's cases, long black braid swaying as she walks. Anu turns, looks back at the market. She looks worried. As they reach the compound, a pack of beggar children surrounds them. Anu shoos them off, but Margaret looks torn. Then they reach the front gate of the compound and the porter lets them in, looking even more relieved than Anupreet that they are back inside the walls.

Though by now Darnsley is likely ready to get back to work, I wait for them to get inside before I follow.

It's been awkward since that day at the camp with Margaret. I haven't done anything about her. I've just gotten better at avoiding her.

Part of me wonders what it would be like. And part of me wants to find out. I could never have Anu, but why can't I have someone? And Margaret is Margaret. Pretty enough. And she's like a lifeline thrown to me from England.

But what if I'm wrong? What if I reach for that lifeline, only to have it pull away? I'd have to let go of one rope—the one I've attached to Darnsley—to grab onto this one. I can't please him and his daughter—whatever that looks like—at the same time. And if she rejects me, her father will hear about it, and I'll have burned both bridges.

But if I do nothing, I may let my best chance to make an ally pass by.

I look at the book in my basket. Suddenly I have an idea.

Maybe it was more than chance that guided my hand to Mr. Browning.

CHAPTER 12

ANUPREET

I take the parcel from the delivery wallah at the front gate. The brown paper crinkles in my hands, the receipt pasted to the surface peeling away at the corners. I pretend it's for me, that I live in this house, that I have clothing delivered rather than sewing my own with Biji. The urge to hug the package to my chest is so strong, but I know it might muss the clothes inside, and I want them to be perfect when I take them to her.

It's been two days since we went shopping, but the feeling of being out in the market is still fresh on my skin.

I worried about going out, worried about what I would tell Manvir and Papaji, but I didn't have a choice, did I? Mr. Darnsley is the head of this household, and his daughter is my mistress. It would have been wrong to refuse them.

But that isn't the whole truth. I can tell myself I was only obeying my employer from here until forever, and Papaji might even be convinced. But honestly I was thrilled to have a chance to go out, unescorted, with Margaret.

We were like friends, she and I. Like when I used to roam the market with Neera, staring longingly at bangles, scraping together our few paisa to share some sweets from the confectioners' stalls. All that was before, of course. Before the scar. And before Manvir did whatever it was he did. Being out with Margaret made me miss my friends, my life before even more, but I loved it all the same.

And the other truth is, I was proud, too, to be with her. Her golden hair drew every eye, and I liked the feeling of being important enough to lead her around the market, to haggle with the merchants for her. Though it was hard not to laugh when she tasted the imli. That afternoon I asked Shibani to make a chutney of it to go with the samosas, and Margaret clapped and shouted happily when she recognized the taste.

It is the kind of thing one friend would do for another.

But friends also tell each other their troubles. And I can't bring myself to burden her with mine. So we are apart in that way, friends but not friends.

Also, no friend of mine has ever spent as much money as she did in the space of an hour. I worried what her father would say, but he took the remaining money and the news that she had also ordered a harmonium easily. Maybe Manvir is right. Maybe all the British *are* rich.

And even though I know it was wrong, even though I know Papaji would be very troubled to hear of even one outing, I hope we have another reason to go out soon.

I carry the parcel up the stairs, following the sound of Margaret playing the harmonium. Her first day with the instrument she was like a toddler learning to walk, but already she runs.

I love the harmonium, love that it's given the house a voice. And Margaret seems so much happier, so I like that, too. Still, the songs she plays are as foreign to me as some of her language. Usually the harmonium sounds sort of sleepy, thrumming along under the words of our prayers at gurdwara or the songs at school. But how could Margaret know ragas or the folk songs? Instead she makes it do strange, wonderful things. The tune she plays as I carry the package into her room bounces and slides, lively.

"Look!" I call out over the music.

Margaret stops, turns from the window where she has set up the instrument to take advantage of the view.

"My clothes!" She climbs to her feet and pounces on the package, ripping it open before she's even laid it on her bed. The two salwar-kameez sets are lovelier than I recall, somehow prettier here in her room without the chaos of the shop to compete with them. And the sari is beautiful, the deep purple blouse and petticoat of lightest cotton. I wish I had such fine things.

"Help me change!" she says.

I rush to shut the door of her bedroom and then cross to draw the curtain. I'm shocked when I turn and she's already out of her blouse. Anyone could have looked up and seen, but she doesn't mind.

"Which one, Anu?" she asks, crossing her arms and staring at her new wardrobe.

I reach out and touch the blue one. "Nilla."

She snatches it up and flips it around, begins to pull it over her head. It's fitted, and I have to help her pull it past her shoulders, but it finds its way into place. Perfect. Margaret sighs heavily.

"So much airier," she says, fanning herself with her hands. "Now the trousers."

She's beaming as she lets her skirt and slip fall the floor, wrestles off the stockings. "Mother can't make me wear these if I'm not wearing a skirt, now, can she?" Margaret smiles wickedly and pulls the salwar on, struggling a bit to get her feet through the bottoms. I help her with the tie at the waist, taking care to not make it too tight.

"Oh," she moans. "It's like a dream, Anu. They're better than pajamas!"

"Very pretty, miss," I say, smiling, reaching for the dupatta and casting it over her shoulders, letting it drape down her front the way I wear mine. *She looks like me*, I think. Or I look like her. Either way, I am happy at the thought.

"Watch this!" she gasps, leaping across the floor, pleased at how freely she moves. I clap and giggle.

She hurries back to her spot at the harmonium, sinks onto

the cushion, sitting cross-legged. "So much easier," she cries. Then she takes back up the jaunty tune she'd been playing when I came in with the package. The music slips around my ankles like water, inviting me to move. So I do. I begin to kick my feet back and forth in steps I've done a thousand times, swing my arms in wide arcs, bob my head. I do not sing as we normally do when dancing giddha, as I would with my friends, but the harmonium is almost its own chorus, filling in for the tabla and the chanting all at once.

Margaret laughs and shouts her encouragement, playing faster. I flick my wrists back and forth, cut my eyes at imaginary dance partners, grin. I'd forgotten how much I'd loved dancing. Almost forgotten how to dance at all.

A shriek from below stairs cuts off the playing and the music abruptly.

Margaret and I rush into the hallway to find Mrs. Darnsley flying up the stairs, breathless.

"They have come!" she whispers in panic, charging for her husband's office like a speeding camel.

"Who, Mother?" Margaret asks as we trail along behind her.

Mr. Darnsley and Tariq are there as a car horn blares from the drive.

We rush to the window.

It's a big machine, certainly beautiful—dark green body panels and a black hood, the windscreen fringed in a thick layer of dust where the wipers cannot reach. I cannot see into the backseat, but the driver is standing half out of the car, one foot on the drive, the other still inside, as he speaks to the guard at the gate. He wears a funny sort of uniform, like one of Mr. Darnsley's suits.

"A Rolls-Royce," Tariq murmurs, staring at the car from the other window.

His voice surprises me. It is gentler than when he speaks to the Darnsleys, trying so hard to sound grown up. Now it is soft, like wind in high branches. He seems surprised too, for he blushes. He hadn't meant to speak, I realize. But he likes this car. Its silver figurine on the hood, the headlamps like buggy eyes.

"Go down and see who it is," Mr. Darnsley orders Tariq. He hurries from the room.

"I know who it is!" Mrs. Darnsley cries as she does up the buttons at the top of her blouse. "The Mountbattens have come!"

I know who the Mountbattens are, knew it even before I began working in this house. They are the most important Britishers in India.

I look back outside. Tariq is in the courtyard now, jogging across the gravel path to help the porter with the gate. The car slides through the opening as Tariq eyes it hungrily.

"What?" Mr. Darnsley asks. "How can you know that?"

Mrs. Darnsley screeches something about that being the only car of its kind in India. We all peer out the windows as it slides to a stop in front of the house. In back sit an elegant, skinny woman and a girl who can only be her daughter.

"The viceroy is not with them," Mrs. Darnsley sputters, sounding almost relieved, "but they have come. And paid *us* a call! Your note must have gotten their attention!"

"What are they doing all the way up here?" Mr. Darnsley asks. Now he's fussing with his clothes, rummaging beneath the maps on his desk for the tie he earlier abandoned.

Mrs. Darnsley turns away from the window, starts to answer her husband, but when she catches sight of Margaret, her face pales.

"What on *earth* are you wearing?" she asks her daughter. She doesn't sound pleased.

Margaret backs away from the window. "I picked it out from the market—it just arrived, it's so much cooler—"

"Go and change at once," her mother orders. "You look ridiculous. First that accordion-piano chimera and now this . . ." She waves a hand at the Margaret's outfit.

"But Mother—"

"We'll discuss the worrisome way you've gone native later. Right now go and change." She dismisses Margaret, then pulls me along behind her down the stairs, whispering orders about tea and refreshment, and warning not to serve those awful pick-led things.

I swallow my disappointment, think better of telling her how much her daughter has taken to the pickled mangoes, and disappear into the kitchen as she sails toward the front door to greet her guests.

CHAPTER 13

MARGARET

This dress feels like a bloody cilice after the deliciousness of the silks Mother made me abandon. Why am I always the one who ends up suffering for Mother's obsession with what people think of us? I sip at the chai Anu has set out. I'd better not mention to Mother how much I've grown to like it, finding the taste of the spices growing familiar and welcome. The sweetness and the cardamom roll together on my tongue, loads better than plain old tea with milk. But if Mother found out she'd surely make me quit the stuff altogether.

Going native. *Honestly.*

"We're quite delighted to see you both," she says again for the hundredth time to Lady Mountbatten and Pamela, who sit side by side across from us on the divan.

"Not as delighted as we are to see you," Lady Mountbatten

says. I like her instantly. With her little white dog she's been slipping bites of samosa to, her face all angles and interesting lines, her limbs spindly but sure, she puts me in mind of Katharine Hepburn in that picture with Cary Grant and the leopard. "We need the expertise of good men like Mr. Darnsley in order to tie this up."

Father hems, looks abashed by the compliment.

"And how pleased I am to see you've brought young Margaret with you," she adds, turning to me. "I'm sure you'll have to come and stay with Pamela in Delhi soon, or even come abroad with us."

I answer, knowing neither will ever come to pass. "Thank you."

Mother, however, is all silent vindication, arching one brow, shooting me her *I told you so* look. She sits taller. "But what brings you here? Your call caught us most unawares."

Lady Mountbatten laughs. "Yes, well, the post isn't quite as efficient here as in England. And I hate the telephone. I've given up trying to warn folk if I'm stopping by. But Pamela and I were on our way to Amritsar to visit a camp there and see how the work is going. You were on our route and we thought we might pop in and see how you were faring?"

"Quite well," Mother says. "Though we haven't been so lucky as you in finding places to help." She tells her about our morning at the camp, the cholera, and how we've been stuck at home since.

Lady Mountbatten smiles sympathetically. "You'll find

something, I'm sure." She is elegant in her own way, in the way that finds its home in someone so direct. There's little that's coy about this woman, and I'm beginning to understand why so many describe her as so beguiling. My eyes drift to her daughter and I search for the same trademarks. She's a bit softer at the edges than her mother, and content to let her carry the conversation. But she holds herself with ease, and her interest in the talk seems genuine. Lady Mountbatten goes on, "I do applaud your persistence. I've always thought the more conspicuously the people see us striving to meet the needs of those suffering, the safer we all will be."

"Of course, Lady Mountbatten," Mother says.

"Edwina," Lady Mounbatten says over her teacup. "Please call me Edwina."

Mother beams and forgets to speak for a moment.

Father fills the silence. "I'm to go out into the hill country next week. Survey expedition. I've been quite cooped here, you see, so I'm very eager to examine a bit more of the place I've come to know through all these maps."

"As well you should. India is remarkable. And those with a keen appreciation of its people and beauty will no doubt do her justice in this difficult business. I told Dickie time and again how shameful it is that we don't have more people to do the survey work. These decisions on the boundary award feel so rushed and arbitrary."

Father nods. He's complained about the same thing. But the

viceroy and the British government have been adamant about keeping to the timetables, about transferring sovereignty on the fifteenth of August, whether they've made a thorough job of the partition itself or not.

Mother reaches for a slice of cucumber on her plate, still glowing from Lady Mountbatten's invitation to address her by her first name. And for all Mother's silly hopes about bringing me to India and making me respectable, it's easy now to see what she was after. Edwina Mountbatten is impressive. I suppose I was expecting a woman who was playing at the role of humble aristocrat, performing her noblesse oblige. Someone doing what she could to look good in all those photographs. I wasn't expecting to like her. Or believe her. Or admire her.

It's inspiring, to tell the truth. And it makes me want to do something as well even more.

"Might you indulge me in a stroll about the grounds, Margaret?" Pamela asks abruptly, setting her chai on the table and looking at me.

"Um . . ." I look at Mother.

Pamela presses on. "It's just that I saw the most beautiful bougainvillea tucked away in the corner of the garden. I'd like to have a closer peek. Would you mind?"

"Pammie loves her flowers like I love my Prince," her mother says, digging playfully into the space between the dog's ears. "We all like something pretty, something useless—particularly in a place like this."

I look to Mother, who realizes I'm still waiting on her permission. "Oh!" she says with a start. "Go! Before the rain starts up again!"

So Pamela Mountbatten, daughter of the viceroy of India, my cousin by too many branches removed, and I leave the room and the shade and the tea and the adults and venture into the garden.

"You don't have a cigarette, do you?" she begs as soon as we're far enough from the house.

And suddenly I like her even more than her mother.

I grin and look back just to make sure Mother and Lady Edwina haven't decided to follow us outside. "This way," I say, leading her to the small bench behind the squat tree in the far corner (opposite the one with what I guessed was the bougainvillea). "Just a tic," I say as I crouch beneath the leaves and lift up a rock as big as my two hands together, revealing the small bowl I've scooped out of the sandy soil.

Pammie gasps. "Brilliant."

"I'm nearly out," I tell her as I fiddle with the lid on the tea tin. Last time I came out for a smoke I had only three left.

"Welcome to India," she groans. "Where it apparently is impossible to find cigarettes unless you're a man who's willing to roll his own."

you. I wish I could be in love. Just once. I wouldn't mind a scandal, even."

I laugh. "The scandal part sounds better before you're in one."

She shrugs as if she's not so sure as she reaches out and takes back the cigarette. "Anyway, I doubt I'll ever get to find out. Mummy seems bent on using up our family's share of indiscretions."

I tilt my head, study her. Wonder how long I'll have to wait before she volunteers the nature of those.

Not long.

Pammie leans in close. She whispers. "She's taken a lover."

I don the appropriate look of surprise, letting my mouth fall open in a pantomime of shock, but with just a half smile curling at the corner.

"Father, too," Pammie says casually. "Several, really. But nothing near as scandal worthy as Mother's paramour. Hers is a bit more platonic than Father's have tended to be, but shocking nonetheless."

"Double standards," I say, then draw on the cigarette. It's half-gone already. "A man can rut about all he wants before marriage, run away and ruin the country girl, and it's quite overlooked, but not us."

Pammie shrugs. "Quite. But Mother's is a bit more complicated."

I wait.

"Hers is Indian."

I pause. "You mean—"

"A native," she says, nodding. "And not just any native, but the most famous one in all of India—"

"Ghandiji?" I gasp. The withered little man in his baggy white dhoti and the movie star–like Lady Mountbatten?

She wrinkles her nose. "Perhaps second most famous."

I can't think of another, my mind still shaking free of the wicked notion of such an odd pair. I shrug.

Finally Pamela whispers, "Nehru."

Now my surprise is real. Completely and utterly real. "The Congress Party leader?"

She nods. "He's a dear, really. And it's not hard to see why Mother's smitten with him. He's no use for Father, and if it weren't for Mother, he'd probably hate poor Daddy as much as Jinnah does."

"Your mother and Nehru—"

"Just letters and long walks and things. But there's something there. Something they might act upon—"

"Girls!" comes my mother's shout from the path leading to the house. Pammie tosses the cigarette to the ground and crushes it with the toe of her shoe as Mother comes into view.

"Ah, there you are!" she says. "Pamela, your mother wants you. Says you two might be off soon."

Pammie smiles, takes my hand, and leads me back to the house, following my mother, who I'm sure is beaming at the notion that

Pammie and I have become such fast friends. But I know better. There's no other girl for Pamela to confide in. Just me.

"Remember," she whispers, "not a word about this to anyone."

"Does it bother you?" I ask her without thinking.

She lingers back, letting my mother get farther out of earshot. "That Mother has a lover or that he's an Indian?"

I hesitate, somehow embarrassed that it's the latter. Fat drops of rain begin to fall. But if today's rain is like the showers that have come before, it will do this for a good spell before dumping out in earnest.

She shakes her head, leans closer, and whispers as if we were the oldest of chums, "In either case, no. And if you could see Nehru, you might forget the color of his skin altogether, if you understand my meaning."

We reach the edge of the drive, several steps behind Mother. Up ahead, Tariq emerges from the house and says something to the chauffeur, who starts up the great motorcar. A slow smile breaks across my face. I take her arm and whisper back, "I think I know exactly what you mean."

CHAPTER 14

TARIQ

The mountains are bigger than anything I've ever seen, and if I stand in the right spot, ahead of Mr. Darnsley and away from his table and transit, I can't see another person or building anywhere. It's amazing, really, being so isolated up here. I know I should be impressed, and I am. But not the way I ought to be.

Not when all I can think about is Anu.

If she were here with me now, I could talk to her. Really talk to her. Not like at the house where no one lets me near her. We could—

Mr. Darnsley's voice breaks in roughly. "Bring me the charts with the water rights," he orders without looking up from the map laid out across the folding table.

I hurry to the car, reach for the map case in the backseat,

and slide the chart from the tube as I walk back to the table. Focus. I must focus.

Darnsley takes the map from my hand, begins to spread it on top of the one he has been studying. I fish around for more stones to hold down the corners against the wind.

"Damn hot," he mutters.

It is not hot. Not really. Maybe to a man accustomed to cool English summers. If I did not worry that it might offend him, I would pull my jacket from my bag.

I fill the cup from the water jug we've brought along, hold it out to him, but not over the table where it might drip on the maps.

Finally unbending from his study of the charts, he takes it and nods his thanks as he moves back to the transit set up on top of its three-legged stand. The instrument is a kind of scope for measuring angles, attached to a rotating base and then mounted on a tripod. Mr. Darnsley explained it to me once and even trusted me to read the tiny numbers that appear inside to confirm his reading. Right now he has it trained on the peak of Arjuna some four or five miles off. But instead of looking through, he stands beside it, gazing up at the mountain.

"Madness," he says, not for the first time as he bolts back the contents of the tin cup. By now I know what he means. Know why he says it as he looks out over the unbroken expanse of foothills and rivers and green valleys, toward the impassable peaks of the Himalayas.

"Mountains like those should belong to no one but God, wouldn't you say, Tariq?"

I look out. Wonder if he cares which God. Start to say so, but instead do what I always do. "Quite right, sahib."

He turns. "For the last bloody time, please don't address me as such."

"Apologies, sir," I say, bowing my head.

"The British are not the rulers of this place," he mutters. "The title is unfit, as unfit as it ever was."

"Of course, sir," I say, and somehow the look he gives me makes me think he's as annoyed by my obedience as he is by the word "sahib." I take a chance.

"It is just . . . ," I begin, "the word perhaps is not so inappropriate as you might believe."

He waits for me to go on.

"It is true that it means 'owner,' or 'master . . . ,'" I begin. "But it also means 'friend.' And it is not a term applied exclusively to the Raj or its representatives."

I've got him now. I go on, careful to temper my accent, measure my words slowly. I sound too Indian when I get excited or nervous.

"The Sikhs use it as a term of respect for their gurus; in Islam we use it as you might call someone 'mister.'"

He considers, his face unreadable. For a moment I am worried I have said too much and presumed far more. To call a white man a friend. But then he smiles. "I believe this might be the first time I've heard more than ten words together from you, young man."

I duck my head. A move I learned from watching Abbu speak with foreigners in the shop over the years. "Begging pardon, sir."

He laughs. "Not at all! I quite like being corrected. So long as it's not on which tie to wear or how high I ought to seek to trade on a name or a connection several men removed."

I don't lift my head. Instead I hide the grin that breaks across my face. I've heard Mrs. Darnsley. Heard enough of her nagging to know that though I may be ambitious, she's a world-beater.

For a while the only sound is the wind riffling the dry grass with the promise of rain that will not last. The monsoon has been odd this year, little storms every other day or so, but the great flood of rains holds off. Ammi thinks the delay is a bad omen.

Darnsley is back to staring at the mountain.

"George Mallory disappeared in the Himalayas, trying to climb Everest," he says.

I've heard about Europeans coming here to climb mountains. I've never understood why until now, when I see them up close like this for the first time.

"Do you think anyone's ever stood up there?" he asks, pointing at the peak.

I shrug. But when I realize he's not looking at me, I add, "I could not say."

"It's impossible," he says finally, but he's not looking at the mountain this time.

"Sir?"

"We're a world away from Jalandhar. Two days in the car brings us here, where there is honest-to-God snow up on those mountains, rivers purer than anything in England."

This is my first time in Himachal Pradesh too. The mountains start here, and all over there are the hill stations the British favored to escape the heat of the cities. The very best of the boarding schools in India are here too. When I was a boy and my daadaa took me to the oratory competition in Delhi where I was the candidate from our sector of Punjab, it was a pupil from one of the fine boarding schools here in Himachal who won. His English was perfect as he recited Keats's *Endymion* as if he'd learned it at the poet's side. He is probably at Oxford by now, that boy.

And me? The judges called my recitation of Coleridge's sonnet, "To the River Otter," "deeply felt," but I didn't win anything. Still, on the train home my daadaa told me how proud he was of me, and how I had honored our family, how I would bring even more honor to them when I went to England for school.

I wonder if I'd gone to school up here if maybe I'd be farther along. Himachal does seem to exist apart from India. I wonder if the people in the tiny villages we can see tucked in the bends of the rivers below even know what's happening in cities around Punjab. After independence and partition, everyone expects the Himachal kingdoms to unite and throw in with either Pakistan or India. Darnsley has been sent to make sure that the crown's maps are current and that they are prepared to revise them properly when the princely states confirm their intentions.

"And they say carve it up fairly," Mr. Darnsley laments, looking away, shaking his head as he returns to the table bearing the maps. "Absurd. Radcliffe won't even come out of his compound in Delhi. And while he's supposed to be listening to our recommendations, I doubt he'd like to hear what I have to say about this."

I wait half a minute before I finally ask, "And what is that, sir?"

He fiddles with the dial on the scope. "There's a story in the Bible . . . ," he begins, before turning to me. "King Solomon. Do you know who Solomon is, Tariq?"

I do. We had a teacher at school who was obsessed with the parallels between Mohammed's holy writings and those of the Jews and Christians. "He appears in the Qur'an. Or someone like him. There he is called Suleyman. A wise and gracious king."

Darnsley narrows his eyes. "King Solomon is in your scriptures?"

I dip my head. "The imam would say Suleyman is in your scriptures."

He laughs again, and I believe I am beginning to understand this man, to perhaps understand the means by which I might appeal to his sensibility, to make him see the right in helping me. Good thing. Sticking with him has fewer complications than whatever I'm trying to do with Margaret.

"Fair enough. Do you know the story of the two women who brought to him a child, both claiming to be the mother?"

I shake my head.

He seems pleased to have an opportunity to enlighten me. "These women appeared before wise King Solomon pleading and screaming, both swearing that the baby they held between them belonged to her. Neither could produce witnesses or evidence to verify their claims."

The wind kicks up, dislodging one of the smaller stones anchoring the chart to the table. I scramble to replace it.

"Solomon," Darnsley continues, "thinks on this for a moment, then he orders that the child be cut in half, one half given to each woman."

I smile now, remembering the story, or something like it.

"One of the women immediately mounts a claim to the upper half of the child's body. But the other is horrified, renounces her claim, and begins to weep anew."

I fill in the rest, the way I used to when I knew an answer in school and wanted to say it aloud, just to impress the schoolmaster. "And Solomon recognized the true mother as the one who would not see harm come to the baby."

He nods, jaw set, eyes troubled.

"It's meant to be a story about how wise Solomon is," he continues. "But I've always thought the mother was the real hero in that tale. The one willing to sacrifice her own heart so that her child might remain whole."

"Certainly," I agree.

He doesn't look at me as he speaks. "They say the people want partition. That it will bring peace. That it will be better in the end. But I keep wondering, waiting for someone to realize that cutting this body in half may do more harm than anyone realizes."

He is right. But I don't know if he wants to hear me tell him so, or if he wishes I would contradict him, reassure him somehow. Luckily, I don't have to decide. A gust of wind tears the map from the table altogether, sending me chasing after it.

The driver spits his words through the gaps in his front teeth, trading on a few Punjabi and English phrases he must know to survive when he speaks to me or Mr. Darnsley. I cringe every time he slips into Dogri to curse the car or call out to another person on the road. Part of me feels like apologizing to Mr. Darnsley for him, and part of me wonders why I'm embarrassed by him in the first place.

I realize it's because I don't want Darnsley thinking I'm like the driver.

But I have to sit in front beside him. Mr. Darnsley sleeps in back.

It won't always be like this, I remind myself. *Promise* myself. Someday I will have men to drive me, the back of a head to stare at when my eyes tire of reading a newspaper.

As backward as he is, I still admire the driver's skill as he pilots the car down the road. He's confident as he threads the car through the narrow gaps in the rock cuts, unfazed as the frame jolts on the ruts or as he dodges a small flock of sheep that appears in the road when we round a bend.

Darnsley sighs and wakes behind me. "Where are we?"

I twist in my seat. "Just coming out of the foothills, sir. I believe the driver will stop for petrol soon, and then a few hours more to Srinigar."

He rubs his eyes, cranks down the window halfway, gulps the dusty air. "Good," he says. "We overnight there and then change drivers in the morning for the trip back to Jalandhar, correct?"

"Yes, Mr. Darnsley."

He drinks from the canteen. "You did a fine job planning all this, Tariq," he says. "Crackerjack efficiency."

"Thank you, sir," I say. Things have gone off perfectly. I'm relieved.

"You have a day off coming when we return, do you not, Tariq?" he asks.

I nod.

"What will you do with your holiday? Have you a girl to visit?"

I shake my head. "No, sir," I say, even as Anupreet dances right into my brain. "No girl."

What would he say if I told him that there were two right

under his roof? He must have noticed Anu himself. Who wouldn't? He'd probably even understand if I told him.

Or should I tell him of his daughter, the way she looks at me? His daughter, who I'd left cigarettes for, and now that book of poems. The thought of what I'd done . . . the risk of it . . . makes me sweat. I roll down the window an inch.

"Quite so," he says. "I expect you and your family are making preparations to relocate?"

I nod. "My father is packing the shop. Some of my uncles have already taken their families. But—" I stop, wonder if the time is right. If I was right about how he was speaking to me on the ridge a few hours ago. There may not be a better moment.

"Yes?"

"I do not wish to go to Pakistan," I say in a rush, glad that the driver doesn't react, grateful that he cannot understand.

Darnsley is quiet a moment, then says, "You would stay in Jalandhar?"

I shake my head.

"Then what?"

I hesitate, look away, watch the trees flying past the windows for a moment before looking back at him. "I wish to study."

He stares at me for a moment, eyes narrowing. "Pakistan will have a university. It seems evident that Lahore will go to the west, and I understand that the school there is very good."

"Of course, but—" I falter. "I wish to go to the best university in the world."

He pauses before he speaks again, as if he's aware of something happening. "What do you mean?"

"I would go to Oxford." There. I've said it now. No turning back.

"Oxford?" he asks, unable to hide his surprise.

I nod, wait. He looks down at his hands, picks at the nail on his ring finger.

"I was at Oxford," he offers at last.

"I know." It was one of the first things I worked out about him when I started.

"But it's so far?" He says it more like a question.

"I have been an excellent student. You only need to ask my teachers from the school. Mr. Ahmed, the one who recommended me for the post with you, he has encouraged me—"

"But Oxford, Tariq?" he says. "What does your family say?"

I swallow hard. My family says little. When I was younger and Daadaa was alive, my parents humored his plan to send me to university abroad. And then after his death Abbu tried to give it up, saying that with the money Daadaa left, I could have enough for any school in India and a bit left over. But I did not want any school in India, and when Abbu realized this, he quit bringing it up. And when I understood that he doubted my ability or the possibility of reaching Oxford, I quit talking about it. I think Abbu figured that meant I'd given it up, but I hadn't. He'd see. I'm so close now.

But Darnsley doesn't need to know any of this. "They understand that my education is important."

"Won't they need you as they resettle?" he asks. "Christ, won't Pakistan need smart young men like you to guide it?"

I wish I could climb over the seat to face him properly. "I believe I could help Pakistan more by getting the best education I can," I say. "The three most important men in the country right now were educated abroad. Nehru at Cambridge, Jinnah and Gandhi both in London." I have imagined giving this speech dozens of times.

"You could do anything in the new country," he says. "A little more schooling and you could teach or practice law. . . ."

This isn't how this is supposed to go. He's supposed to offer to give me a reference, to help me. Instead he's trying to get me to change my mind? "But the men who lead, the men who decide the fate of the continent—"

"Have emerged out of a British patriarchy," Darnsley points out. "But the country is changing. What the British value won't matter as much anymore." He says this as if he is not one of them.

"But—"

"No, Tariq," he says. "You don't need Oxford. But your countrymen will need you."

I stop, turn back around, and stare at the road beginning to straighten out in front of us. My stomach suddenly feels empty and heavy. The air in the car is close and sour.

What's happening? Heat rises up the back of my neck and burns my ears, my face. How can he do this to me? How can he refuse to help without even thinking about it? Maybe his wife is right about him. Maybe he *is* without ambition. How else could he dismiss mine so easily?

"Oxford would ruin you," he says. "You're too good for it."

Ruin me? *Ruin me?* I want to put my fist through the windscreen of the car. Maybe then he wouldn't think me too good for it. Or maybe I should tell him about the man I probably killed. Or maybe I should tell him how I think about his daughter, how easy she would be . . . I'd heard enough of her fights with her mother about someone called Alec to know it wouldn't be that hard. Not doing something about how I felt for Anu is *lohe ke chane chabana*. Like chewing iron pellets. Doing something with Margaret would be easy.

Would that make him think me better suited for Oxford?

I bite the inside of my cheek. I taste a bit of blood.

"You belong in India," he says with finality, landing a blow more decisive than any punch I could throw.

"Pakistan," I correct him, unable to keep the anger out of my voice.

He falls silent behind me. Maybe he's embarrassed at his mistake. Allah, I hope so. At least let me have that.

CHAPTER 15

ANUPREET

"Mother!" Margaret is shouting again. "Mother!"

I leave the tandoor and the chicken roasting inside and sidle to the back door. When Margaret shouts, I'll be expected soon.

She's been funny lately. Moody. I sort of wondered if I'd done something to make her upset. I couldn't think of anything and figured I was just being silly.

I'm sure it has to do with missing her father, with the house being so quiet with him gone. But she makes it even quieter, playing her harmonium less than before, and the songs she picks aren't much for dancing.

Instead she spends almost as much time reading as she used to devote to playing.

And every time I see her, it's the same book. The little yellow one Tariq left in her room before they drove off last week.

Margaret had been downstairs with her mother, saying good-bye to her father. The car, loaded with Mr. Darnsley's equipment, rumbled in the driveway, waiting. I had gone upstairs to shut the curtains in Mr. Darnsley's office, and as I passed by Margaret's room, I saw Tariq standing there, holding something in his hand.

Keeping to the shadow, I'd watched him a moment. His back was to me, shoulders rounded, tense. He'd jumped when Mr. Darnsley called up from the driveway, telling him it was time to go. Then he had sighed, whispered something to himself, and bent down quickly, placing the skinny book carefully on top of Margaret's harmonium. I'd ducked into the back room as he turned and bolted down the stairs.

I'd waited until the sound of his steps had faded, until I could hear the car pulling away. Then I went into Margaret's room to look at the book. The title was in English, so I couldn't read it. A few minutes later, when Margaret came back upstairs and found it, she'd asked where it came from.

"Tariq," I'd told her.

"Tariq?" she'd said. "You're sure?"

"Haan. I saw."

Her smile was so small it was like a secret. But she liked the gift. And I supposed it meant she liked the one who gave it to her.

I hadn't thought much about Tariq like that. But I could see then that maybe Margaret had. It made me nervous, but I wasn't sure why. And it also reminded me that we weren't friends the way friends really are. We leave too many things unsaid. I didn't tell her about my brother, about his injuries or how long he was taking to heal, or how I worry what will happen when he does. She didn't confide in me about Tariq.

"Mother!" Margaret shouts once more.

"Why must you carry on like a common thing!" Mrs. Darnsley snaps from the opposite end of the house. "Half the neighborhood can hear you!"

"Most of them don't even understand me!" Margaret snaps back, but they've drawn closer, one standing at the top of the stair, the other at the foot. They don't shout any longer. "It's my hair again."

I creep to the doorway leading from the kitchen to the hallway. Old Shibani—the Bengali woman who is the housekeeper—told me when I started work here that my job was to be never seen but always at the ready. I've made a game of it. Trying to be where I know I'll be asked for, trying to surprise my employers with my sudden appearances.

"Your hair?" Her mother sighs. "Honestly, Margaret!"

"You'll be the one complaining if I can't mend it!" she says, and I silently agree with her.

Rather than argue, Mrs. Darnsley does what I knew she'd do the moment Margaret began shouting. "Where is the girl?"

"I'm sure she's busy in the kitchen . . . ," Margaret begins.

"I haven't time to help you again." Her mother begins to edge toward the dining room and the table where she's set up her own desk. "I've letters to post and some telephone calls to make. And I still have to plan tonight's dinner with Shibani—"

"But, Mother . . . ," Margaret begins, her voice gone high and wavy.

"Don't be silly. Let the girl do her work," Mrs. Darnsley says, walking away. "Anupreet!"

I wait a moment, telling myself that just because Margaret wants her mother to help her doesn't mean she doesn't want me. Does it?

I find her in her room—a room that is as big as all the bedrooms in my house—at a table with its own glass, a dozen vials and combs and pots piled amid hairpins scattered like so many grains of rice. I can see myself in the little mirror hanging on the wall above the table as I come in and stand behind her.

I'm so plain next to her. So dark. So small.

"It's the heat, Anu," she complains, clawing at a knot at the end of her hair with the brush. "And the infernal dust. Bloody mess is all knots and tangles I can't work out. It was difficult enough at home, but this place is altogether awful."

She doesn't meet my eye, but once again I'm struck by the color of the mass that she curses. And the curls are so fine—like each strand has its own direction.

I feel the heavy black braid at the back of my neck, know that if I unwound it, my hair would hang straight and dull, black as old coals.

"My salheri has such curl," I say. "We must oil."

She looks at me curiously, wrinkling up her nose. "Oil?"

I laugh. "Wait here."

I hurry down to the kitchen. On the shelf above the basin, I reach for the pot of coconut oil. I take the stairs two at a time back up to her room. Margaret sits where I left her.

"Only a little," I say, opening the jar, dipping two fingers into the paste. The oil is soft, like set ghee, a bit runny at the edges. I scoop a portion no bigger than a quarter-anna coin.

I don't wait for her permission as I massage the oil between my palms, then begin to rake it gently through her curls.

She is silent as I work, half watching the window that overlooks the front courtyard, half watching me. In a few minutes I've worked out the knots and tangles. In a few more, I've used her combs and pins to settle the curl into place. The curls are perfect, easy waves, like the swirl of cream that stands on top of dal makhani before serving. My belly rumbles. I must be hungry.

"My," she says, turning her head from side to side.

I step back.

"Thank you, Anu," she says, looking briefly at me.

"I help you dress?" I ask her. She is wearing one of her salwar-kameezes. Mrs. Darnsley gave up fighting so long as Margaret promised not to wear them outside the house. But it is wrinkled where she's been sitting at the harmonium, and damp at her back with sweat.

"Actually," she says, rising, going to the wardrobe, and opening the door, "yes." She pulls out the purple sari. I gasp at the sight of it. It is so beautiful, and Margaret will only make it even prettier. Somehow, if she wears it, it feels as if things will be all right between us again.

I shake out the blouse, the silk fine and perfect in my fingers. I hold it open to her as she sheds her shirt and underthings. She slips into the choli and buttons up the front. It doesn't pull or gap across her chest, the sleeves just right on her upper arms, the length hitting just so at her ribs, leaving the flat of her belly and navel exposed.

"Oh bugger, I'd forgotten how short the tops are meant to be," she says, spreading her hands wide across her bare stomach, trying to cover it up. "Mother's going to have a bloody stroke."

I stifle a giggle. Mrs. Darnsley might, but I suspect Mr. Darnsley will be pleased. He, at least, seems to like India. He relishes the curries we serve. He has encouraged Margaret's playing at the harmonium. I find myself hoping the sight of his daughter in so beautiful a sari will make him proud.

"Nice," I say, reaching for the petticoat. Margaret hesitates, mutters something about "Romans" that I do not understand, and drops her salwar to the floor, stepping into the petticoat. It too fits perfectly. Then I reach for the sari. I gently unfold it on the bedspread so as not to trail it on the floor, removing it from its tissue wrap. I've only worn a sari a few times, for special occasions, but I've known how to drape one from the time I was small. When we were very little girls, Vineeta and Neera and I would turn even a tablecloth into a sari, dressing up and pretending to be glamorous ladies. I wrap the fabric once around her, tucking it into the waist of the petticoat, making sure that it falls all the way down to the floor.

Margaret watches me closely as I turn her back around to face me, adjust the fabric in the front, and begin pleating. I make six perfect pleats, each the depth of my hand, falling in easy drapes to the floor. The silk is even better than I realized, holding the shapes I coax it into. Margaret keeps her arms lifted over her head, but she stares at my hands as they fly across the fabric.

"I'll never be able to do this myself," she says.

I smile but think that anyone who can play the harmonium as she does can surely make a few pleats. I will teach her next time. But now I'm too eager to see her finished in the sari to wait. I tuck the pleats carefully into her waistband, just to the left of her belly button.

"Almost done," I say. I take the rest of the length of the sari and wrap her once more, bringing it back around to her front and then lifting it across her chest, letting the pallu fall over her shoulder to the floor, where its end lies perfectly flush with the bottom edge.

I stand back, smile, and nod. "Now you are cooking with gas," I say, borrowing one of Margaret's odd phrases.

She laughs, rolls her eyes at me, and crosses to the mirror. But when she sees herself, I can tell she is surprised. She grows still, her shoulders straighten, and she lifts her chin.

"Oh," she says, reaching up to pat her hair, as if to make sure the girl in the mirror is her. The pallu slips from her shoulder; she lifts it back up, but the silk slides down again. "This thing is worse than the dupatta," she grumbles. I cross to her dressing table, find a pin, and solve her problem.

The gate creaks at the street as the sound of a car draws closer.

Margaret turns from the mirror, glances toward the sound. "They're back!" She says it urgently, and I think how she does love her father. She's watched the windows in anticipation of his return. And why shouldn't she? I can't imagine coming so far from home and then being left with just her mother in this giant house, in a place where she cannot even go out. Not when she's come from London and worlds I can't imagine, glamour and faces as beautiful as hers, where apparently her hair behaves all by itself.

Yes, I think, she loves her father, as I love my papaji. I used to wait for Papaji to return from the shop, hiding in the low branches of the mango tree. I used to love to call out to him like a bird when he reached the door, or drop down on him like a leopard. I was just like Margaret, so excited her father was coming home, even if it was only after a day of missing him.

But then she leans into the mirror, rubbing a bit of something pink across her lips, pinching at her cheeks with both hands before standing back to survey the front of her sari.

That, I think, *was not for her father.* And I realize that was for *him.*

Tariq.

"You're a dear, Anu," she says, winking at me as she walks carefully to the hall, pouring down the stairs in ripples of purple silk. I cross the room to watch from her window as she steps into the gravel, as her father emerges from the car.

Mr. Darnsley shouts in surprise and delight at Margaret's sari, lifting her arm and twirling her around once, twice, before bowing low to kiss her hand, both of them laughing. She swats at his shoulder and steps in to kiss his cheek. I watch her hug him, but I see something else, too. I see the way she looks over her shoulder at Tariq. He's tugging long leather cases from the rear of the car, unstrapping a trunk from the top. He doesn't seem to notice Margaret's eyes on him. Doesn't seem to notice anything but the work he has in front of him. He begins to carry the cases inside, without even looking up at Margaret. Her father has released her and is speaking with the driver now.

Margaret is still standing in the drive, still at her father's side, but her eyes keep flitting from the tire of the car to the door Tariq slipped through. I hear him on the stairs now, the cases thumping against the wall every few steps.

Then her mother appears and shrieks in a way that's nothing like her husband's happy cries of a moment before. She stomps to her daughter like an angry elephant, grabs her hand, and nearly pulls her off her feet as she hurries her back into the house.

I pull away from the window before I am seen and grab

the pot of coconut oil. I steal down the stairs and back into the kitchen, replacing the pot before Shibani has a chance to see it missing.

Margaret and her mother are arguing quietly in the sitting room. I hear her father join them, trying to soothe Mrs. Darnsley's fury.

Shibani is still not in the kitchen. I open the wooden door to the cooler and pull out the clay pitcher of lemon water she made this morning. Three cups wait on a tray above the basin, clean. I fill them from the pitcher, the cool liquid already sweating against the sides of the glass.

Mrs. Darnsley may not like the sari, but I think I'll be safe in bringing them all something cold to drink. I lift the tray and turn to make for the hall but find Tariq blocking the doorway, watching me.

"Oh," I say.

He doesn't move. He doesn't smile, or speak.

He just stares.

I gesture with the tray toward the hall and the Darnsleys beyond.

Tariq keeps looking.

I remember Manvir's warning, how I'd just thought he was being overprotective, like always.

But what if he wasn't?

Because Tariq *was* looking at me now, in a way Manvir wouldn't like. In a way I don't like.

The glasses on the tray shimmer a little.

"Sat sri akal," I whisper, ducking my head and moving for the gap between his left side and the door.

"I'm thirsty," he says in Punjabi. I rarely hear him speak anything but English, as most of his talking is with Mr. Darnsley. Now his voice sounds different. Insistent. Almost angry.

He looks at me, his eyes drifting over the kitchen behind me, perhaps searching for a reason to stay where he is, blocking my way. But those eyes always find their way back to me, and it begins to make me nervous, his looking. The kitchen suddenly feels small. I have to get by, to take the water to the Darnsleys, to Margaret.

Margaret. An odd pang of guilt stabs at me.

Tariq's eyes travel down from my face to the tray in my hands. He reaches out and takes a glass. Lifts it to his lips and drinks deeply, his eyes on me all the while.

And for some reason I feel something strange. The way he looks at me, the way he sees me, maybe. There is a flare of something that calls back being in that shop, with that shard pushed up against my cheek, another man's eyes staring wild at me.

Another Muslim.

I feel the panic rustling inside me.

He starts to put the glass back on my tray, but I shake my head. Move again toward the door.

He does not budge.

Already I'm wondering how I will avoid telling Papaji of this, whatever this is, when he comes for me this Sunday. Wondering what I will say.

Tariq edges forward. "How old are you?"

But another voice breaks over him from behind.

"Anu?" Margaret barks. She is standing in the shadow of the hall behind him.

Tariq straightens, bows his head, and bolts out the back door, cup still in hand.

Margaret takes another step, the silk of the sari swishing the only sound. "Anu?"

I hold the tray out to her; she looks at the cups as if they might be poisoned. I catch her staring, look down and see what she must be seeing. Two cups, and the bright wet ring remaining from the one Tariq took.

She draws herself up, eyes looking down on the top of my head, and steps aside.

"Father is parched," she says. "They've gone out to walk the garden. Go."

And I'm too relieved to have escaped the kitchen to worry about what she might think of me now.

CHAPTER 16

MARGARET

I stand in the shadow of the doorway, watching Anu serve Mummy and Daddy the drinks. She seems calmer now than when I found her with Tariq. But she won't look up at my parents, only bowing humbly, taking the glasses back from them, waiting there, staring at the the tray. My parents don't seem to notice her as they walk the long way through the garden to the little patio off the downstairs parlor, disappearing inside, Father remarking how nice it feels to stretch his legs after all those hours in the car.

But Anu remains glued to the spot, fixated on those cups on the tray. She is breathing too quickly, swallowing hard, and she stays that way until the old housekeeper appears, chattering at her in Punjabi, and shoos her back into the kitchen.

"Anu?" I call out. My voice sounds sharp, sharper than I mean it to.

Her head jerks up, eyes wide, like she's just woken up from a bad dream.

"Are you all right?" I ask. I'm not sure if I'm jealous or annoyed or worried or what for her now.

It's terrible, this feeling. Of liking Anu but at the same time sort of resenting her. It makes me feel small and mean inside, but I can't help it. I can't stop myself from looking for flaws or vanity or meanness, like what's inside me, though I've never seen it. I can't help it though.

But I know others simply can't help watching her, period.

Then again, it's not like I caught her snogging Tariq in the kitchen or anything.

But then I think of the way he was looking at her.

A way he's *never* looked at me.

Ever.

Suddenly I feel like a trussed up cow in the sari, almost as embarrassed by it as Mummy was. What could I have been thinking? *He* didn't even seem to notice. What a yuck I am.

Anu's standing beside me now, staring at her feet, holding out the tray with the two empty glasses and the one remaining for me.

"Are you all right, Anu?" I repeat.

She nods, keeping her eyes down. I can almost see my reflection in the shine of her hair, and I wonder if someone oils it for her as she did for me. I take the glass from the tray.

"Thank you," I say, sipping small before putting it back.

She disappears into the kitchen. I feel a little badly for how meekly she's carrying on now, but fine, then, here it is: Part of me feels justified. I've eyed a fella before only to have him fall for one of my friends. Alec was the only one who seemed to see me and only me. Nadine was there that first day at the hospital when I met him, and all the GIs were forever chasing her, but Alec set his cap for *me*. And sweet Saint Peter, it was wonderful.

Then again, it's not Anu's fault she's pretty any more than it was Nadine's, but still . . . it stings. And makes me in this getup even more silly. I am a ridiculous thing, wearing ridiculous clothing, in a place where I've nothing at all important to do. Ridiculous.

And the feeling is so overwhelming, like a sudden downpour, that I make a decision. I follow Anu into the kitchen where she's washing the glasses at the basin. She looks up like a kicked dog, so I force a smile at her, grab one of the clean kitchen towels from the stack in the corner, lay it out flat on the counter, and look around. I grab a couple of the bananas, fetch out three of the hard-boiled eggs from the icebox that Mother asks Shibani to keep on hand for her breakfasts, nick a handful of the parathas left over from lunch, and then dump the whole show onto the towel. It doesn't look like much, so I dash up to my room, snatch a few of the paisa coins from the little bowl on my dresser, and skip back down the steps. Anu is drying the glasses now, slowly. I can feel her watching me. The coins clink merrily as they settle in with the bundle of food. I draw the corners up, tie them across the middle and lift the makeshift picnic.

Anu clutches the dish towel, her mouth set. She knows what I'm up to. I raise a finger to my lips and sneak out the back door.

The sun is high overhead, baking the gravel hot enough to fry bacon if you could find it here. I fiddle with the latch on the door leading to the alley, have to lay down the cloth bundle to work the bolt free with both hands. Once outside, the rubbish heap is just there to the left of the door. It smells a bit whiffy, and I reckon from the scraps of bread near the edges that the boy hasn't been here yet today. I look about, realize with a delicious sense of freedom that I'm *outside. By myself, and without permission.* I'm also doing something other than whingeing about having nothing to do, so I'm feeling aces all around.

I place the bundle carefully on top of the pile. My little friend in the green top is nowhere to be seen, but I feel confident he'll find it, and even more confident he'll know who put it there. I duck back inside the door, throw the bolt, and turn to find Anu, arms crossed.

"Oh, don't be such a stick in the mud," I say, knowing she won't understand the idiom. But I don't care. And I'm not worried. We'll keep each other's secrets, she and I. That's what friends do, after all. I squeeze past, sail through the kitchen, and float up the steps. I start for my room, but Mother's voice from Father's office catches my ear.

"But a dinner party is—"

"Out of the question!" Father says back. "Besides? Who could we possibly invite?"

"Perhaps some of the other men working on the boundary award," Mother suggests.

I watch from the crack in the door, see Father shaking his head. "Half of them are in Delhi, and the other half are scattered across the Punjab and Bengal. The nearest other man is in Amritsar—"

"The Mountbattens, then," Mother says, spine stiffening.

Father laughs. "I don't think we'll entice Dickie all this way for supper. Invite the Lady and Pamela next time they're on one of their relief errands, but I'll thank you not to embarrass yourself by asking the viceroy to stop for tea in the middle of breaking the subcontinent in two."

"But—"

"But nothing," he says, stalking from the veranda and into the parlor, straight to the cigarette box. "To say nothing of the risk of it all. Half a dozen British surveyors in one place would make a lovely target."

"Don't be ridiculous." Mother waves her hand as she follows him inside, but she doesn't sound convinced.

He struggles with the lighter. "The only reason they don't come after us is because we're scattered. If we look like a tribe, if we assemble together, then . . ."

Mother is quiet, filling in the blank for herself before she dares speak again. "You're being dramatic. What would they want with a few surveyors and cartographers?"

He eyes her, inhales the smoke. "You know Radcliffe?"

Mother nods. "By name only, of course. If we had a party—"

Daddy cuts her off. "He never leaves his compound in Delhi. Our communications are given to guards at the gates who then carry them to him. Only rarely does he even permit an audience—"

"He's a barrister from London, for God's sake. The king is less anxious—"

"But he's the closest thing to a face this whole mess has. The lightning rod for all the anxiety and fear about how this world might be cleft in pieces. There are death threats every other week, already a couple of crude bombs heaved over his walls. Somebody boxed up a snake the other day and had it sent to his house! Can you imagine? Assassination by snakebite?"

Mother sounds annoyed. "Why are they troubling that man while the viceroy sails around the countryside like a movie star?"

"Mountbatten is the man who's giving India back to India," Father explains. "He's the smiling face of the British Raj backing slowly out the door."

Mother settles back into her chair, defeated. And looking at her there, I almost feel badly for her.

I push open the door and edge into the room. "Mother?"

She turns, rolls her eyes to find me still in the sari. "*Please* go and change," she begs. "I've conceded to the pantsuits but can't allow all this bare skin at your belly." She looks up, surveys my curls. "Your hair looks divine, though."

I touch it. "Anupreet did it." I don't rat her out about being the one who wrapped me up in the sari. It wasn't her idea, after all.

She nods appreciatively. "The girl is a wonder. I swear I'd pack ten of her to London if I could. And at the pittance we pay her, I could nearly afford to!"

"Lucinda!" Father says sharply.

My stomach tightens at the thought of an army of Anupreets marching down London's streets, bewitching every eye in sight.

"Mother . . . ," I begin again. "I was thinking, now that Father has returned, now that things will likely settle down, I'd really like if we could try again at being useful here."

Mother's eyes soften; she smiles at me. "I'm so glad to hear you say so, pet . . . ," she begins, "but I've had no word indicating that the cholera situation is improving in any of the camps nearby."

"What about someplace else, then?" I say, kneeling beside her. "An orphanage, maybe." I'm almost intoxicated with the idea of doing something more, what with leaving the food in the alley for the boy. I'd like more of this feeling.

She hesitates. "An orphanage," she says, tilting her head, turning the idea over in her mind. "That might be just the thing. There are hundreds more orphans now with the population exchange in full swing. The poor little things keep getting separated from their parents." She squeezes my hand. "Why didn't I think of that?"

I'm too happy to have pleased her that I don't point out the reason she didn't consider it: There haven't been any photos of Lady Mountbatten visiting orphanages in the papers back home. But I'm sure the papers won't mind a change of venue.

"That's very thoughtful of you, Margaret," Father says, but the look he gives me is more suspicious than proud.

I sit. "So long as we're here and you're working so hard, the least we can do is mitigate some of the suffering the empire has caused."

Mother's smile melts away. "Keep your politics out of it. We'll help the suffering—never mind the cause," she says, adding, "As if we induced them to burn one another's houses down and kidnap their daughters—"

She doesn't finish as the first of several cries interrupts her. A battle cry, like the ones from war films, rises up to the open veranda doors. Then more cries ring out, this time ones of surprise and fear and pain.

I fly to the veranda, crowding Father's shoulder even as Mother orders me to get out of view, her hand on my arm to pull me back, but even she freezes at the sight of the street beyond the walls of the compound.

A mob is moving upon the market—the very one Anu and I visited. Men stream from two narrow lanes like water into the maze of stalls. They wave sticks above their heads, a few rattling kirpans—the curved sword Anu told me the orthodox Sikh men wear.

"What's happening?" I whisper. But I know—it is a riot. And

I know by the turbaned heads that the mob is mostly Sikh men, and I remember from my visit with Anu that the vendors in this small market are predominantly Muslim. I don't ask because I don't know. I ask because I hope I am wrong.

"We should move away from the windows," Father advises, but he seems as transfixed as I am. The first thing I'd noticed upon arriving in India were the crowds—the constant crush of people on the streets, in the shops, moving around the city. I'd begun to grow used to them, the throngs, the constant noise and movement. But this is different. It's shocking to see so many moving together, in one direction.

And for the first time, I'm a bit frightened. Frightened at the thought of that mob shifting toward our house, of the stream being diverted toward our crumbling wall and the gate with our single guard. What would a guard do against a hundred men or more?

And I wonder about the truth of why England is giving up India after all these years.

Can it be because they're frightened too? There are thousands of soldiers and diplomats still here in the country, but even with better arms and defenses and power and gated homes, there is no shelter from hundreds of millions of people if they refuse to cooperate.

And I think with a start what it might mean if they disapprove of the lines Father and the other men like him will draw.

There is movement at the other window. Tariq is peering

through the curtain. He sees the turbans and the short blades flashing overhead just as I do. I know precious little about him, but I do know that he is Muslim. I try to imagine what it feels like to watch his own people being overrun. The roofs of the market stalls, most of them canvas tenting or cheap planking, begin to ripple and buckle as the mob cuts its way through. And from the other direction I can see the rush of bodies tumbling out of the market, some clutching parcels and bundles to their chests.

Father looks over to see Tariq staring. "I think—" he begins.

"It's all right, sir," Tariq says, stepping back. "The mob will not come this way."

I wonder what makes him sure, what makes him confident enough to make such a pronouncement.

"No, I don't think they will," Father says, though he sounds doubtful.

"It's appalling," Mother whispers. "Really, what makes people behave so?"

No one answers, least of all Tariq.

Father and Mother turn back to the windows, but my eyes are still on Tariq. He continues staring out the window, and I watch him for signs of outrage or empathy or anything, but his face is unreadable.

And then quickly his eyes dart to mine, and he looks at me. Really looks at me, instead of through me or around me as his habit seems to dictate. Those amber eyes lock upon mine, and hold me there.

I've heard there are serpents here that immobilize their prey simply by staring at them, that the strike is almost secondary. And I think I might know now what it feels like for some smaller animal to be caught in the gaze of the cobra.

Tariq continues to look at me, even as the noise increases outside, as the smoke from the first of the fires rides in on the breeze. And his expression is as impenetrable as ever. He might love me or hate me.

But he is looking.

CHAPTER 17

TARIQ

Almost before the riots in the market even quieted, I turned to Mr. Darnsley and asked to go home.

"Are you sure it is safe?" he asked, eyes taking in the damage across the street.

"They will not trouble with just me," I said. But the truth was, they might. Or another pack of men might. But I didn't care. I could only think of Ammi and Abbu and Arish and whether they were all right.

"Of course you may go," Mr. Darnsley said, and I bolted from the room.

I ride fast, faster than I usually do on errands for Darnsley. But it takes me longer to get home, because I keep taking side streets and long-cuts. I don't want to risk running into a riot.

Ya Allah, I wish my brain would stop churning. I wanted to

feel fury at what I saw the Sikhs doing at the market. I *should* feel fury. But instead, all I can think about is how *I* had done the exact same thing at the mosque—the exact same thing. We are all doing the exact same terrible things.

Maybe I do belong here after all.

Maybe this is how Allah is punishing me. Maybe Mr. Darnsley refusing to help me is part of that punishment.

I *have* to get out of India. *Have* to get to England. Though I know even England isn't far enough away for me to escape my shame. But now I know for certain that I will come back. Now more than ever, I believe this. I'll come back and they'll have to listen to me. Just as they listen to Jinnah. I'll help it stop, this fighting.

Will they listen to me? A man whose hands are as dirty as anyone else's? I have to hope so. I have to try.

I have to get to England.

When I finally make it home, the house is turned inside out. Blind panic seizes me for a second as I think the mobs have come to our neighborhood, but then I see that only *our* house looks different. "Ammi? Abbu?" I shout, swinging my leg over the seat, barely slowing down enough to keep from crashing into the gate.

"Tariq!" Ammi rushes out toward me, and before I can even push the bicycle inside, she wraps me in her arms. I return her hug with one hand, the other balancing the bicycle. The chain presses against the leg of my churidars, and ridiculously

I wonder how long it will take me to wash the grease stains from it before I have to present myself to Mr. Darnsley in the morning.

"I'm all right, Ammi," I say, resting my chin on top of her head.

She lets go, looks me over, and decides I am telling the truth.

"Chalo," she orders. "Come. We've much to do."

I follow her inside. The furniture is mostly gone. Wooden crates filled with straw form a maze on the floor.

"We will store them in the mosque until we can send for them," Ammi says.

"Abbu means to go now?"

"On the Friday train," she says.

Friday! Three days?

"Why so soon? Was the shop looted?" I ask with alarm. Our shop is in the fanciest market, far from where the riots have been so far, but—

"Nahi," she says, "but it is only a matter of time. Unless you pay the bribes for protection, they will come. But there is no sense protecting what we must give up eventually. He says Pakistan is the only home for us now."

Pakistan. I can't go to Pakistan. I can't leave. Not now. Not while there is still a chance.

Margaret will help me. Please, Allah, make her help me.

I have to tell them. I've waited so long not because I'm afraid of disappointing them or scaring them, or that they'll forbid it, or any of that. All those are givens. Those things won't change no matter what moment I choose to tell them.

No, I haven't told them yet because I know it will hurt. Hurt them. And me. Already I feel my heart breaking a little and have to clench my fists to keep my hands from shaking. But there's nothing for it. I have to tell her now. No way out but through, Abbu would say.

"Ammi . . . ," I begin, swallowing hard. "I do not want to go."

Her eyes soften; she lifts a hand to my cheek gently. I don't think I can get through this if she tries to comfort me now.

"It is hard, Tariq," she says, looking from my eyes to the boxes, the crates, "to leave so much behind." She knows as well as I do that the chance of these things she has spent a lifetime collecting and using probably won't make it to Pakistan. "But at least we will be together."

I shake my head, her hand falls away. Just tell her! Just say it! "I will not go."

Now Ammi looks at me, eyes narrowing. "Tariq?"

"Pakistan has nothing for me," I say. And as I say it, I realize how hard it sounds. The shock in my mother's eyes betrays how much I have hurt her.

They will be in Pakistan. All my family will be.

"Tariq," she repeats, unsure of what else to say.

I hear my father at the gate, hear him call my name. He carries a paper bag in his hand. "I saw your bicycle outside. . . ." He sounds relieved.

"There were riots in the market across from the Darnsleys' house."

"Riots everywhere—" Abbu says, shaking his head.

Ammi interrupts. She cannot help herself, cannot keep the words inside any longer. "Tariq refuses to come west with us."

Abbu drops the bag on the floor, the contents rattling and shifting inside. It sounds like he has a pile of pebbles within. His eyes are wide, worried. "What is this she says?"

I feel all the careful arguments I've prepared abandoning me. When I rehearsed them in my mind, I wasn't staring at Abbu's stricken face, or Ammi's tears. It wasn't supposed to be like this.

"I have a chance," I manage, my voice breaking, "to fulfill Daadaa's dream."

"Daadaa?" he says, confused for a moment before I see understanding wash over him, and then something like grief replaces that as he says, "Oxford?"

I take a deep breath, nod. Abbu thought I'd given it up.

"Oh, Tariq," Abbu says. Ammi wails softly.

I shake my head. His voice is too gentle. It would be easier if he didn't pity me now. Easier to stand my ground.

"I know you want to honor your grandfather's memory. But if he were alive now, he would already have taken us to Pakistan."

"But I—"

He steps closer. "You can go to the university in Lahore after we settle. Already you have more than enough learning to run the business or be a teacher, to be respected. You will do us all great honor—"

"I will do us more if I can get the education that forces men to listen to me." I wish I could make him understand that *enough* in his mind is a scant portion in my own.

"My beta." He steps closer, lowers his voice. "You won't need it. Pakistan will be different, you see? We go to a place where a man can start a life for himself, free of oppression, free of the threat of an ignorant majority. A place where work will equal success."

"I can't," I say. "Not yet." Tears sting at my eyes. I'm almost as sad that I can't see Pakistan as he chooses to as I am to be hurting him and Ammi.

He turns, speaks to Ammi, an edge of frustration creeping into his voice.

"I should not have allowed this job," he says. "The poison of the Britisher! It eats at him! He cannot return to that house."

"I have to!" I say. "They need me." And I need them.

He looks at me again, softer this time. "We are khandaan," he pleads. "There is no need greater than that, is there?"

I hang my head, study the fraying edge of the rug under our feet.

Abbu goes on. "You know what we have done for you? For your brother?" He holds up his finger, retrieves the bag from the floor. The bottom sags, the contents rattle as he reaches for my hand.

"Abbu—"

He hisses, cuts me off, and into my hand he pours a mixture of gleaming stones. Even in the dim room, they catch the light, twinkling like stars against my palm. There are diamonds, small ones, chunks of gold like clumps of rice, and rubies.

"It is the only way to move our wealth to Pakistan." He glances about as if the walls have eyes and ears. "And it is dear enough and unsafe enough as it is. But we take everything so that you and your brother may prosper, may find good wives—"

I bite my lip as I pour the stones back into the bag, but still I say, "No, Abbu." I think of my brother, wonder why he isn't here to see this. Maybe all this wealth will make some father look past his half a leg and give him his daughter, anyway. It will be easier if he does not have to share it. And Arish—he can run the shop on his own.

As if he reads my thoughts, my father says, "He cannot do it without you."

"Arish is stronger than you think."

Abbu suddenly looks as if he wants to strike me. I edge backward. "And you?" His voice is a challenge. "Are you stronger than I think? Do you know what it will be like to be on your own?"

I say nothing. I've thought about it. But now, with telling them, it starts to become even more real. Distance seems to spread out between us even while we stand here. And it hurts. It hurts much more than I thought it would.

My doubts start to scream louder inside my head. The scale

of what I'm planning threatens to overwhelm me. It would be easier to go with them. So much easier to obey.

But I know I'm right. I know one day Abbu will be proud of me for standing up to him. And prouder still when I come back.

"I have to try for Oxford." It feels smaller and more foolish each time I say it aloud. Like I've said, I'm going to fly to the moon.

He throws up his hands. "Your grandfather was an old man, Tariq. His dream of Oxford—"

"*My* dream," I say.

He lets it pass, shakes his head. "And what will you do when you reach England? How you will pay for Oxford? I don't expect they give degrees away—"

"There is Daadaa's money—"

His hands tighten into fists. "His money?" he says. "The money he left wouldn't be enough for passage on a ship! I told you before. He was an old man. His mind was not right. He had no notion of how great the expense was."

"But . . ." I am stunned, but the way Abbu says this, I know he is telling the truth. He wouldn't lie, not even to get me to come with him.

"There is not enough," he says more gently, sensing an opening. "There is enough there for a year, perhaps two at the university in Lahore, but certainly not enough for England—"

He reaches out a hand and places it on my shoulder, consoling me. But I shake it off, angry, furious. Why won't anything work out as I plan? I needed more time, time for Abbu to get used to the idea of going to Pakistan without me. And I'd counted on the money my daadaa left being enough. *But there are other ways*, I tell myself. I cling to the thought like an anchor before I speak again.

"I will work. Mr. Darnsley will help me find a position," I lie. I do not tell him he has already refused me, that my only prayer now is that he will not refuse his daughter.

"Darnsley?" he spits. "This man presumes to help you? Against my wishes? To break up a family?"

I can't say more, don't dare let him see how full of holes my plan is.

His expression shifts from anger to grief, his shoulders fall. "Khandaan, Tariq," he begs. "It is all that matters, is it not?"

I swallow hard. "Abbu, I can't go," I repeat.

And now there is fear in his eyes. "But it is not safe—"

"Neither is the journey to Pakistan," I point out. "Anything can happen on the way—"

"But we will protect each other." He reaches for my mother, whose tears fall freely now. He holds out an arm to me.

Part of me wants to give in. All of me wants to hold them, tell them everything will be fine.

But it won't. Either way, there are risks. Pakistan is no surer than England.

I could make them feel better. For the moment. I could pretend to let him win. I could go along with their preparations to move, and then just slip away at the end, duck out of the train as it leaves the platform. It would be easier.

But only for me.

"I'm sorry, Abbu," I say simply, choking on the words. Ammi's knees buckle under her and she falls into my father. He grabs her, but I back away.

"Tariq!" Abbu thunders. But I'm already running out the door and into the twilight, my father's hands reaching for my kurta hem, my mother's cries trying to pull me back.

I vault over the gate, leave my bicycle behind, and run halfway down the block at a sprint, making my lungs burn so my eyes won't.

As I reach the corner of the lane, I crash into someone coming around the corner. I bark out an apology and make to keep running before I see who it is.

Sameer. My heart sinks even lower. He is everywhere these days.

"My friend," he says, almost warmly. "I heard that your family leaves soon. I have come to say good-bye."

I feel my jaw tighten, afraid that if I tell him, I won't be able to hold myself together. And Sameer is the last person I want to cry in front of. I swallow hard, try to think of something to say, but am distracted by a flash of gold at Sameer's neck. A thin chain dangles there, tucked beneath the collar of his shirt. Sameer has never had more than a few rupee to line his pockets. But now he wears gold?

I study the chain, fixing on this detail. Focusing on it helps me ignore the urge to run or scream or break down and sob.

Gold?

Could it have something to do with what he was doing in the market last week? I start to ask him, but then I reconsider. Telling him what I saw could go badly for me. So I stand there, mouth hanging open, the words crawling back inside.

"You will go with them?" he asks.

My family, I realize. He is asking about my family. "Nahi," I manage.

"They will go without you?" he asks carefully.

"Haan," I say, and I realize what it means for the first time as I say it aloud. My family will go without me. Even if I try to catch up with them later, it could be almost as impossible to find them as it is to get to Oxford. I heard enough that day at the camp to convince me of that. And those were families who traveled together before they were attacked by dacoits, or simply got lost in the great columns of people migrating back and forth.

But it's a risk I have to take. "My work keeps me here."

He nods as if he understands. "Ah, yes. We are alike, this way. I cannot go to Pakistan yet either."

This is as unexpected as the gold chain around his neck.

He shrugs. "My family has already gone, what's left of them," he says. The smile holds fast, but there is a knife's edge in his voice now.

"But you stay?"

He lays a hand across his chest. "Like you, I still have much work to do."

My eyes find the gold again. I wonder how he has found a way to make his version of *work* pay.

"So we stay here together," he says, "behind enemy lines, as it were?"

I say nothing, kicking at a skeleton of a palm leaf on the lane.

"Who knows? Maybe our paths will cross as we fulfill our obligations?" he presses.

I look up sharply.

"Many men I work with will be very pleased to hear that you remain in your position," he says. "Men who, when we arrive in Pakistan, will see to it that you and your family may not struggle as other families will—"

"I'm not going to Pakistan for a long time," I blurt out. As soon as I say it, I with I hadn't, wish I hadn't given him some reason to question my loyalty.

But he takes it in stride. "Perhaps these same men might be induced to reward you and your family in other ways, then. Perhaps they can help you get where *you* wish to go. Wherever that may be."

And I remember. I remember when Sameer and I were something more like friends. When we were at school together. When I might have told him that someday I would go to Oxford. That someday I would matter.

And I see in his eyes that he hasn't been collecting information all these years out of idle gossip. He's been amassing it as currency.

I've just given him a small fortune.

I know I shouldn't ask it, but I can't help it. What if they *could* help? What if they could get me to Oxford somehow? "What would I have to do?"

"Simply be ready," he says easily, taking a few steps away. "Ready to assist your countrymen and claim your reward."

He smiles, pats my shoulder, and stalks away.

By the time I wind my way back home, my brother is outside.

"Tariq," he says in a way that tells me he's been waiting. He sits on a wooden chair, one leg of his trousers tied into a neat knot, tucked up inside itself, hiding the stump of his leg. One hand rests on that leg, the other drums away at a small bundle of black cloth in his lap.

"Arish," I say. There is no second chair, so I drop down on the ground and sit. Since he came home injured, I have felt ashamed of myself for standing over him.

"I was on the roof before," he says. "I heard you arguing."

I hang my head. We are quiet a long while, listening as the city settles, both waiting for the other to begin.

"I've spoken to Abbu," he says finally. "He's agreed to let you come later."

I stare up at him in surprise. His face is half in darkness, the other half lit from the lights within the house. He shaved recently, a bright red scab of dried blood highlights his jaw.

"Later?"

He looks at me, his voice firm. "You cannot stay in India forever."

I lean forward. "I don't plan to stay in India—"

"I heard your plan," he says quickly. "If you can call it that."

I say nothing.

"You're insane," he says, "if you think a Britisher will take you home with him. I lost my leg in their war. They called me a hero."

I drop my head again, stare at my hands. My parents pleaded with him not to enlist. The same way they begged me not to stay just an hour or two ago.

"But what did it get me?" he asks. "The British soldiers I served with, if they went home to England with an injury like this, the government gave them something. Some money or a job. But not us."

He is quiet a long while, fuming. I know this silence.

"We get nothing. As if our limbs are worth less because they are brown," he finally spits out. "Our lives."

"You were a hero," I say after a beat. I have to say it even if I do not mean it. Even if there is nothing heroic at all in letting yourself be used in the way he has.

"What I *am* is a cripple." He shifts in his seat, lifts the leg with his free hand. "But I will not be a burden to you. Besides, you *should* get more education. Do you know who the safest men in the army were?" His question is a challenge. I don't bother guessing. He presses on, leaning forward in his chair, the wood creaking with his weight. "The officers. And do you know what most of the officers had in common?" Again, I don't interrupt. "Papers from Cambridge, or Oxford. They weren't the best soldiers, weren't even the best leaders, but they were too damned valuable to be allowed anywhere near a German bullet like the rest of us."

"Arish—" I'm ashamed now. Ashamed that I've thought these same thoughts. To hear him speak them makes me see how wrong it is, how wrong I might be for wanting to be like them.

He silences me with a wave of his hand. "And make no mistake, there will be war for years to come. Do you think all this between the Sikhs and us will die down when we have a border?" He shakes his head. "How much worse will it be when there are real boundaries to dispute, real territories to squabble over? Already there are rumblings of what will happen if Kashmir goes to India—"

"I don't want to fight," I break in, "I want to study."

"When you come back to Pakistan"—his tone dares me to contradict him—"they will want you to fight. But if you have the right degrees, the right knowledge"—he reaches up and taps my forehead hard with two fingers—"they will at least let you fight from a distance."

He extends his hand, holding out the bundle of cloth from his lap. "Here."

I take it, feel its weight. I know what it is without even opening it.

"Your knife?" I say. The trench knife was a prize he took off a tank gunner, the only material thing he brought home from Tunisia. I have heard the story a thousand times, watched him sharpen the blade, oil the leather sheath with the snap across the handle. I unwrap the bundle and run my thumb across the grip, the little swastika inlaid in the butt of the handle. The Nazis stole the swastika as their emblem, but it was born in India, where it brings good fortune. Arish knows I need luck more than I need the knife. But so will he.

"I can't," I say, returning it to him.

"You'll need it more than I will," he insists. "If you stay. If you follow us to Pakistan later."

"But—"

He shakes his head. "It's yours now. And if you persist in a fool's hope, one that will trap you here and put you at the mercy of the Sikh mobs . . ."

My brother is trying to protect me.

"But what will you do?" I ask, scrambling to my feet. I tie the leather thong at the top of the scabbard around the drawstring at the waist of my churidar, then tuck it inside.

He laughs. "If we even make it to Pakistan alive, and with Abbu's money still with us, I can run a shop from a chair as well as any man from his feet. I'll manage."

"Abbu agrees?"

He hesitates. "I've convinced him you will not desert us."

He doesn't sound sure as he says this. Or proud. Or protective. Or frustrated.

He sounds resigned.

He stands, leaning on the crutch he retrieves from the floor. "Write to me from London," he says. "If by some miracle you make it there."

I nod. My eyes well up again. This time I let them fall. I'm ashamed to cry in front of my brother. But I can't help it. We both know that a letter has little more hope of finding him after we part than I do of making it out of the country alive.

This may be the last time I talk with my brother. I may never see him again. The possibility of it lands squarely on me, like a punch to the stomach. Suddenly I find it hard to breathe.

Arish waits for me to settle down. I smear the backs of my hands against my eyes, press them hard there, trying to stop the flow of tears.

My brother is patient.

When I finally get my breath back, when the tears seem to have retreated for now, he speaks.

"It is brave, what you are doing," he says, adding, "stupid, but brave, still."

"Shukriya," I manage.

He shakes his head. "Who knew my brother the scholar had such fire in him?" He leans on my shoulder. "Just be sure to bring it back to us in Pakistan," he says, his voice breaking a little.

We stand like that a little while before he asks me, "Are you ready?"

He doesn't have to spell out what he's talking about.

It is time to say good-bye to my parents. Perhaps my last good-bye.

I am not.

But I let him lead me to the front door anyway. For the first time in a long while, I am leaning more on him than he is on me. My right shoulder digs into his side, his hand steering me toward Abbu and Ammi.

And with every step, I am grateful for the feel of the knife there at my hip, the rough stitching of the case scratching at my leg. A distraction from the pain of saying good-bye, a secret bit of my brother the warrior to keep with me.

CHAPTER 18

ANUPREET

The train is late.

We are crammed onto the platform at the station, elbow to elbow with hundreds of others—family members, business-people—awaiting the noon train from Amritsar.

But it is nearly three in the afternoon now.

The Darnsleys gave me the morning free when Papaji walked me back to work last Sunday evening. He explained that our family was to come from the west, were to resettle with us, and that he would like it if I could come and greet them when they arrived. Mr. Darnsley was very kind to let me go.

But now I am worried as we await the train, worried the Darnsleys will be wondering why I've not yet returned.

And I feel awful that I think about this, awful that I fret about disappointing my employer when I should be worried about what all the others around me on the platform are anxious about.

The train.

Trains are often late in India. I've heard Mr. Darnsley complain about it more than once, though that doesn't surprise me, the way that the Darnsleys seem so obsessed with the timings of things. Always taking their lunch at one, dinner at seven. And both Mr. Darnsley and Mrs. Darnsley have made fun of the way that appointments for telephone calls or meetings here seem to be more suggestions rather than actual agreements.

But we Punjabis are not so preoccupied with time, particularly with trains that can be delayed for so many reasons.

An operator who turns up late.

Cattle lingering on the tracks.

Engines broken down.

Anything.

Everyday things.

Until there were other reasons a train might be late. Reasons a train might not arrive at all.

We have heard of things happening.

Of trains being stopped by piles of rocks or logs on the tracks, only to find out that the rocks and logs were put there, placed by gangs of men who then swarm from their hiding places. Gangs who steal. Steal from the passengers who have bundled up all they hold most precious, sold everything they own to make a new start in a new place, only to have it taken from them before they even reach their destinations.

They steal people, too.

Women and girls, my age, older, younger. They are taken. *Used.* Bought and sold.

That happens sometimes.

And sometimes even worse things. There were rumors about a train that reached Lahore filled with Muslims moving to Pakistan. It arrived at the station carrying nothing but corpses.

After those rumors reached us here in Jalandhar, two gurdwaras were burned down.

"Something's wrong," Manvir says again. It is his first time out of the house since his trouble. He was well enough to leave his bed last week, well enough to stand and walk about the garden. But his face is still a sight, a roadmap of yellowing bruises, cuts healing slowly over, his nose cricked to the side now. He cradles the arm in its wrapping against his chest. The doctor has said it will be a few weeks more before the bones heal.

"We don't know yet," Biji says, but she doesn't sound convinced. Even Papaji looks like he is losing hope. The four of us crouch together on the platform, huddled around the tiffins filled with food Biji brought in case Uncle and his family were hungry when they arrived. And though my own stomach is hollowed out now, as all of ours must be, I can't even think of eating.

I hate this feeling. This fear. The dread. The feeling like something is stalking us from the shadows. A tiger about to spring. It's there, I know it, can feel it like eyes watching me, but I can't do anything to stop it.

Across the platform, a few people linger around the ticket windows and the station manager's small office. Two policemen wander up and down the edge of the platform, their heavy clubs bouncing against their legs.

Suddenly a young man wearing a telegram office cap and uniform bounds up the steps, sprinting for the ticket windows. A hush falls on our side of the platform as every head lifts, every eye falls on him. He looks in briefly at the ticket window, but then continues around to the manager's office door, knocking once.

He glances across the train tracks briefly as he waits for the door to open.

And in that moment, no one needs to read the telegram to know what it says. His eyes are wide and sad and frightened all at once. He wears no turban. He might be Muslim like Tariq.

The door opens and he all but throws the telegram at the stationmaster, bolting from the platform, disappearing down the steps, no doubt hurrying to his waiting bicycle.

I watch him disappear and then turn back to the stationmaster. He is opening the telegram. It takes him ages to rip the edges and unseal the message. I may imagine it, but his hands seem to be shaking. He looks across the platform toward us, where we wait with the other families. Then he looks back to the telegram for a moment before his eyes flick back to us. Nervous this time.

All around me, men are rising to their feet.

"Read it!" a voice demands.

Manvir is on his feet. Mother is already crying. Father's hand is across his mouth.

I watch the stationmaster. His face is grim, but unsurprised. He shakes his head softly.

And wails like I've never heard—louder than any train as it pulls into the station or screams out its departure—erupt from the crowded platform all around me.

We are all forced to stand as the crowd edges closer. Biji scrambles to grab the tiffins and find her feet. Around us men begin calling for quiet.

"Read it!" More voices take up the command until the rest of the crowd falls silent, waiting, listening.

I cannot see the stationmaster anymore, but suddenly all goes deathly quiet and still. I look up at my brother, watch his eyes as he watches the other side of the platform, as he listens.

The voice is faint, as if the man cannot muster the energy to shout loud enough to project the bad news. But we can hear him all the same, and the quietness of his voice only makes what he says surer, sadder.

"Train reached Amritsar behind schedule, stop. Most passengers aboard dead, stop. Some wounded, stop. Many missing, stop. Conductor spared to bring train and bodies off the line, stop. Western line suspended until further notice, stop."

And with that, his voice stops. It all stops. And we all stop hoping.

The cry that rises up now is part mourning, part bloodlust. It is fierce, this sound, echoing around the station, the silenced tracks. Papaji links arms with Manvir and Biji and me as the crowd begins to move, some falling to their knees, keening, others racing for the way out of the station, to the streets.

Manvir starts to pull away.

"Son—" Papaji grabs for his hand.

"Take Anu back to the Britisher's house," Manvir demands. He has never spoken to Papaji this way.

"Son," my father repeats, this time a warning in his voice.

"It will be safer there for her," Manvir explains, his voice softer. "Behind the walls, she is safer. We know what is happening to girls all over the Punjab. We cannot protect her here until the borders are closed. Until every Muslim is shut away on the other side."

"No!" I say, my own tears starting to fall. They will not need me much longer. The family will leave as soon as the work is done. "Don't send me back," I say. "Not now."

I look at Biji, whose eyes are clamped tight, like when she has one of her headaches, and she tries to blink away the light, tries to turn day into night to ease the pain. She will not take part in the argument between my father and her son.

Manvir is resolved. "There is no need for you at home," he says, "particularly now. And Uncle's money is no doubt gone with him. The little you earn is even more important—"

Papaji looks at my brother as if he is a stranger. "How do you speak so?" He tilts his head to the side, face ashen. "Our blood is spilled upon a rail bed, and you talk of money?"

"I talk of living!" Manvir shouts. "And living is both the best revenge and the best way to honor those who are gone!"

I take a deep breath, shudder, and realize that he is right. But I also know that there is the hint of more than this kind of revenge on his mind.

"Anu will return to that house. She will stay as long as they will allow her to. Until it is safe," Manvir repeats.

Father doesn't even protest this time.

"Manvir . . . ," I begin. I want to tell him about Tariq. About his stares. But what would I say? What harm has he really done me? And what harm could he do in that place, of all places? Biji and Papaji have enough to worry about, enough heartbreak to mend without me giving them more to fear. So I don't tell.

"Take her back," my brother repeats, edging away. Papaji lunges for him again.

"Where are you going?" he asks.

Manvir hesitates, his voice is even, factual, and it chills me to hear him. "Our people have been slaughtered. And now we must avenge them."

Suddenly I think of my cousins. Little girls. Half my age, Biji said. Perhaps they were excited to ride the train on this journey, as I was excited the day I rode in the car. It makes my insides twist and roll to think what might have happened to them on the line to Amritsar, only a hundred miles or so from the home they left behind.

When I think of them, part of me does want to send Manvir out to avenge our people.

But then another image breaks in. The sight of all those Sikh men raiding the market that day across from the Darnsleys' house. Their kirpans raised. Those were our people too. Our people who slaughtered merchants. Robbed stalls. I know the old men in the gurdwara—the ones who loosen the belts that hold their ornamental kirpans when they sit down to eat langar—they like to go on about the proud tradition of the Sikh to defend the defenseless.

But what happened in the market, was that defending someone? Is what Manvir means to do now defending anyone?

I study my brother again. His face is empty, like the engraving of the British king on a half-rupee coin—expressionless, unmovable. But there is something in his eyes.

Fire.

And I think I can almost hear his mind moving. Not just moving but planning.

Biji's voice breaks in, steadier than I expect. "But when will it be safe? When will it stop? Why will it end when there are borders to separate us? Why?"

And even Manvir, who seems to have all the answers today, has no answer for this. Instead, he turns and joins the army of men pouring into the street.

CHAPTER 19

MARGARET

I've been at the harmonium now for over an hour, my legs growing stiff from sitting cross-legged for so long. I've set it up in front of the window to try and catch a bit of the breeze as I play. My left hand works the bellows while my right hand climbs up and down the keys. The notes may be Chopin's, but the sound is anything but. Anu told me that the harmonium is used in her temple, and I can imagine it right at home in a worship service. There's something even more meditative about it than the piano, the way the notes slide into each other, the steadiness of the sound.

It certainly helps me think.

I'm tired of trying to translate the sheet music I brought with me to the harmonium. It's more fun to just play the tunes I remember, to adapt them by ear. For the last half hour I've been trying to piece the melody to "But Not for Me" from that Judy Garland picture I saw last summer. I keep playing the same phrase over and over, but I'm not getting much closer.

I don't mind. It passes the time.

Nearly a month has passed since the riots in the market across the street. The violence ebbs and flows at random, like the sudden downpours of rain that come nearly every day now. But they are brief, the relief from the heat fleeting, as if the real monsoon is still waiting for something.

Father and his colleagues have been sending frenzied telegrams, shouting into telephones riddled by terrible connections. And as near as I can tell, it's the same elsewhere as it is here. Not in the south, mind you. The south of India might be a different planet. But all over Punjab, and in the east, near Calcutta where East Pakistan will be born, things are the same.

The boundaries are nearly done. I've seen the lines on Father's maps, watched them shift over the last few days, studied the lines that have been rubbed out, the ghostly marks still there like fading scars as new lines are drawn.

Father and the other cartographers and civil servants have been hurrying. No one wants to wait to find out how long it will take for the people to tire of attacking one another, before they come after the remainder of those who've been withholding their independence all these years.

Despite my brainstorm about going to an orphanage, Mother has now abandoned her schemes to improve me through social activism. Angry mobs scare her as much as the threat of cholera, and these riots hit a nerve with her. She'd get this way at home, too, when the bombs fell. They could hit the other side of London and she'd be fine, but when they were close, she'd keep us bound up in the house for days. Apparently she'd have me alive and soiled rather than dead and redeemed. That's something, I suppose.

But I still do what I can. She's not so scared that she's banned me from the garden, which means I can still sneak out to leave my little presents for the boy. The other afternoon he waved and bowed to me from the rubbish heap. And one morning I found a beautiful little bouquet of flowers, shaped a bit like daisies but a screaming shade of pink, in the same spot where I'd left a little pot of cooked rice and chicken the night before. I put them in water but they wilted inside the house before the day was out.

Anu hasn't left the house lately, not even for her Sunday afternoons off. These days her family comes here, standing at the gate with her, or picnicking in a corner of the garden for a while before parting again.

But even when they visit, there is a sadness about her that troubles me. I've heard Mother and Daddy whisper that she's had some family tragedy. I overheard them talking about it a week or two ago, but when I walked in and asked what they meant, Mother got quiet and Daddy just said they were talking about what a pity it was Anu had that scar on her face.

I tried asking Anu myself what was wrong, why she didn't

go home at the weekend anymore. She pretended not to understand my question, though I'm sure she did. She just didn't want to tell me.

I didn't push the matter. I was worried about her, but I was dead distracted, too.

With Tariq. My hands fall still for half a second. Then I break into the second act of *Tristan und Isolde*. Wagner's perfect on the harmonium, all those tritones and the unfinished cadences. They sound even more romantic, even more longing on this thing.

Oh, Tariq. When I think of him, picture his face, I get all woozy and fluttery inside—as I used to when I thought about Alec. He's so gorgeous. And so tragically serious all the time. Like Mr. Rochester in *Jane Eyre*, only without all the money or the shouting or the bossing me around, the way Edward did with poor Jane.

But also like he can't quite figure out what to say to me.

I bungle the third phrase completely, but I keep playing.

We have our secrets, Tariq and I. I've taken to edging nearer the house when I go out to have a cigarette, just so I might see him as he comes and goes on his errands for Daddy. Just so he has a chance to see me smoking the Luckies he gave me. They still haven't run out. A couple of times a week, I'll find one or two new ones.

And then there's the book.

That *book*.

I found it right after he and Daddy left for the north. Robert Browning. It made me blush, to read just the cover. *Men and Women.* Alec never would have bothered with poems.

I play a little louder, give up the bellows for a second to tinker with the stops in the middle to see if I can pull a little more soul out of the instrument.

I knew Browning from school, of course. And the first poem in there was a torcher, for certain. At least the title was. "Love Among the Ruins." Even though the ruins in the poem were likely in Italy or some other place, I couldn't help thinking it wasn't a bad description for what India was crumbling into.

It spooked me, honestly, how bold a declaration it seemed.

But then the rest of the ones in there were confusing. Frustrated artists, dark towers, mad-scientist Arab doctors, and more. I read them all, poring over them, wondering as I read each one what he'd meant in giving them to me.

I was all set to ask him about it when he came back. And then I surprised him and Anu in the hall.

There was something in the air that afternoon. A charge. Like a bomb about to go off.

I'm playing too fast. I rein the tempo back in.

Since that day, he's gone out of his way to be kind to me. Almost bashful. Before, he ducked in and out of my father's office, always eager to return to his side, completing whatever errand Daddy assigned him as quickly as possible. But now— even as Daddy's work reaches fever pitch—he lingers. Takes his sweet time in the corridors, or in the courtyard, and often it feels he is looking for me.

But not always. His eyes still pull toward Anu. But then, everyone's do. . . .

And after all, it's not her he's giving presents to.

But still.

It's funny, all this. The way I'm holding back.

Being careful.

Wary.

This feels different than it did with Alec.

I botch the trill, go back and do it again.

Maybe I'm just older.

Wiser.

I didn't worry about scandal before, or second-guess myself.

Bells, falling for a boy was loads more fun when I wasn't so barking suspicious.

Because I am, I realize. Falling. For him. And how could I not? Wise or not, careful or not, he's something . . . something worth thinking about.

I slide from Wagner into a bit of "April in Paris." I play it nearly all the way through before a noise behind me shakes me out of my trance.

Tariq is standing there, looking caught out. He's about to put something on the small table by the door, but he withdraws his hand, holding it up to his chest quickly, gives that little bow. He's wearing the same sort of outfit he always does, the long kurta, this one in sort of a pearly gray, over the pants that taper and gather at his calves and ankles.

This is the first time I've caught him in the act of delivering one of his little gifts. He's getting bolder. Finally.

"So sorry to bother you," he says, smiling. It's a nervous smile, but still a cracking good one. His hair is longer, curling more at his ears and his temple. It suits him. I wonder if my own hair is as frizzy as it usually is by this time of the afternoon.

"It's all right," I say, twisting around and folding my knees together, sitting up a little taller.

He swallows. "You play very well." He jogs his head to the side, in that way they do here. I still don't know what the gesture means, but he seems sincere.

"I'm no great shakes," I say.

"The music you play is very beautiful," he speaks slowly, clearly, tamping down his accent.

I smile. "I wish I knew some of the local things." I fiddle with the stops. Why am I so nervous? "I've even tried to find some things on the wireless." I point toward Father's office where the radio is. "But I can't seem—"

"There is no harmonium on the radio," Tariq breaks in. "It is against the law to broadcast it."

"Against the *law*? How can you outlaw an instrument?"

"A few years ago all the people with the Quit India movement worried that the harmonium was too Western. It was brought here by . . . by . . ." He pauses, rolls his hand in the air, searching for the right word. After a tic he snaps his fingers. "By the missionaries a century ago."

I look down at the instrument. "Too Western?" I repeat, incredulous that the very thing that seems like the voice of this place had been brought here by Europeans.

"The ban is only on the radio, Miss," Tariq says reassuringly. "And no one takes it too much to heart. The harmonium is too common to truly forbid."

"Well," I say, fiddling with the stops on the front of mine, eyeing the pearly elephants inlaid on the red lacquer. It looks a far cry from what a missionary might have hauled over from the continent, and I wonder how long it took this thing to evolve into its present form.

I hear Father cough loudly in the next room. Tariq starts, as if remembering himself. "I have dispatches," he says, patting the satchel he wears over his shoulder. "Excuse me?"

I shrug. "Cheers."

He nods back. "Cheers," he repeats, placing the little object in his hand on the table by my door. He bolts out of the room and down the stairs.

I'm desperate to see what he's left me this time, but I don't let myself rush there. Instead, I turn back around, floating in the wake of the longest bit of a waffle we've exchanged yet. Granted, the history of the harmonium wasn't the most romantic of topics, but I don't care. I slip back into "April in Paris" and try not to watch the window—I don't want him to think I'm too keen.

But I can't help it. I can't stop peeking out . . . looking for him in the courtyard below. My fingers miss the eighth note when I see Tariq wheeling his bicycle to the front gate, glancing over his shoulder, and waving up to me. I look down just in time to avoid him catching me watching, but I'm grinning like a fool as I play the next measure without giving in to the need to know if he's still looking up at me. When I finally glance back, there is Anu rounding the corner of the house, her arms laden with a basket full of wet laundry.

Tariq watches her for a tic before he pushes down hard on the pedal, launching himself out into the street and the shadows of the afternoon sun. But only for a moment. Good.

I abandon the song, the harmonium wheezing into silence as Tariq disappears into the street. On the table next to the door is the bit of waxed paper he left. I pick it up, unwrap it, and find a small square of chocolate, the first I've seen since we arrived in India. I inhale the scent of it and smile. Chocolate was still hard to come by even at home when we left. I have no idea how he got this, here of all places. It's already starting to go a bit runny at the edges, the lump softening in the heat, so I pop it into my mouth whole. I don't know if it's because it's been so long since I had any or if it really is made differently, but it doesn't taste like any chocolate I've ever had. A bit saltier, but smoother, too. It melts on my tongue too quickly, leaves me wishing for more.

The flavor lingers in my mouth as I head over to Father's study. He's leaning back in his desk chair, eyes shut, rocking slowly back and forth, the spring squealing pitifully with each bounce. The brass fan hums at his feet, tilted up, but his hair stays plastered to his forehead by the heat. The open collar of his shirt flaps in the breeze.

He looks older than he did two months ago when I arrived. He was thinner then, but now he looks knackered. The last ten days or so, with the riots and the hurried work to complete the maps, have taken their toll.

My foot squeaks on the polished tile.

"Meggie." He doesn't open his eyes.

"How did you—"

"You have a way of appearing as soon as I send the boy away," he says, now looking at me with a smile.

I blush, collapse in the chair, hope he chalks it up to the heat. "I find it so dull," I confess. "If only Mummy had let us go see about the orphans."

"Things didn't work out the way your mother anticipated," he concedes. "Though they rarely do," he adds, smiling more to himself than to me. "But not to worry, we'll be going home soon."

I sit up. "How soon?"

He smirks. "I've just sent Tariq to the courier. He'll hand off my final reports and they'll go to Radcliffe. But they're a formality, really. The borders have already been decided. Independence in Pakistan comes tomorrow, here in India on the fifteenth. Then Mountbatten will publish the boundary a day or two after that."

"We're leaving," I say quietly. When I got here, I couldn't wait to go home, but now . . . now. I've barely even seen India, barely seen what it's really like. Apart from that day in the market with Anu, our one trip to the camps, and what I've been able to see from inside this house, I haven't seen anything.

But that's not what really bothers me about leaving. I'm thinking that it seems far too soon to go now that Tariq is warming up to me.

"Within a week, perhaps," he tells me.

"It seems abrupt, now that it's here," I say.

He leans forward, his voice playful. "A moment ago you were telling me how bored you are, and now you want to stay?"

I shake my head. "I suppose . . . Well, this is going to sound silly, but I'd just like to know what I'm leaving."

He sits back, drops his chin, and looks at me as if I've just said something brilliant. "I think I understand."

I peel myself off the chair and go to the window, where the air is fresher. "I wish *I* did."

"India is a confusing place," he says, "and I'm not sure I understand it better for having seen more of it than you have. But someday I'd like to come back. I'd like to come and see that the people have made a go of independence. That it will be safe for everyone when our work has had time to take hold."

"It's just that London seems so far away," I say, trailing off, twisting the muslin hanging at the window.

When he realizes I'm not going to say more, he speaks, and

what he says shocks me. "Did you know that the boy asked me to bring him to England?"

The fabric knots itself around my fingers. "Tariq?"

He swings his chair back to the desk, begins tidying up papers. "Wants to leave India. Or doesn't want to go to Pakistan, rather."

"Why not?" I ask. My heart begins thumping wildly in my chest.

Tariq wants to leave.

He wants to come to England.

I think of a passage from one of those poems he left me.

> *I and my mistress, side by side*
> *Shall be together, breathe and ride*
> *So one day more am I deified.*
> *Who knows but the world may end tonight?*

He wants to be with me. He wants to be with me! And the sureness of it fills me up so completely I think I might split in two.

Father is speaking.

"Are you listening, Margaret?" His voice comes louder now, like I'm swimming up from underwater.

"Hmm?" I manage, without facing him. I can't look at him. Not now, not when I'm sure what I'm feeling is written all over my stupid face.

"I said he wants to go to Oxford," Father says, lifting one eyebrow. "Imagine."

I freeze. But . . . No . . .

Oxford. In an instant it all makes sense. The linen from the curtain is all bunched up in my hand now. I shake it free, take a steadying breath, and face Daddy. "He asked you?"

Father shrugs. "In so many words. He says it is the best way to help his people, that the real leaders of the subcontinent have been educated there."

Oxford. And suddenly I'm ashamed. Ashamed of myself for not even considering that the boy might have ambitions. That he was perfectly content to fetch and carry for a white man because that's the way it's been here for ages.

But just as suddenly I'm angry. Angry as I begin to knit together what Tariq—with his smiles and the presents—is likely to have been playing at in the last weeks. "When?" I ask.

"Sorry?" Father says.

"When did he ask you?"

He hesitates, thinking. "Ages ago. When we were coming back from the survey trip."

The very day he cornered Anu in the kitchen. He'd given me the book the week before, when they left.

"What did you tell him?" I ask, though I already know.

Father scratches at a bite on his wrist. "That I couldn't help him. That he belonged here, that the people of India and Pakistan didn't care anymore for the trappings of British status . . ." He trails off like he doesn't believe it very much himself.

"Is that true?"

He rubs his eyes, stands. "I don't know. Probably not. I don't know how a place can exist for a century with one paradigm and suddenly liberate itself it for another. I don't know."

He's right. I think about how at school they changed the name of the chapel when some old spinster left a load of money to the school. They named it after her, even had a ceremony and a new sign and everything. But we went right on calling it Shepherd's Reach, or just the Reach, like before, even though the teachers all wanted us to honor the lady who'd left all that money by calling it after her name. But pretty soon even the teachers forgot, and it was like it never happened, apart from the sign, at least.

"Old dogs, new tricks," I say bitterly.

"You may be right," he says.

After a long silence I have an idea so utterly mad that I seem incapable of keeping it shut up inside. "Would you help him?" I demand. "If you had reason to?"

"Reason?" He looks at me curiously.

"What would be a reason?" I press. "What would be enough?"

He hesitates. "We've no business upsetting the way of things here."

I laugh. "Honestly? England's been mucking about here for centuries upsetting the way of things. What harm can one person do?"

He opens his mouth to speak, but then shuts it, considers. "I suppose that's so. But it doesn't seem right, somehow. As long as I'm drawing lines on maps, as long as I'm not dealing with faces, it seems quite the thing to do. My duty. But playing fairy godmother to a boy with outsized ambitions is another thing altogether."

I want to ask him why they're outsized. I want to know what makes Tariq so different from Father. What makes Tariq so different from me? What makes him less deserving of a spot at Oxford than any other man?

But the words stick in my throat, held there by another thought: *Why do I even care?*

I'm still wondering when my father swings back to his desk, begins stacking papers into neat piles. We're done talking about this. Whatever *this* is.

I begin rounding up the pencils and erasers and drafting tools, sorting the equipment into ordered groups.

Something catches my eye.

A small brass medal on a tricolor ribbon sits inside an open velvet box, atop a letter bearing the seal of the viceroy.

"What's this?" I ask, reaching for it.

He looks up. "Ah," he says, bemused. "My commendation. Lord Mountbatten's letter thanking me for my service to the empire and a medal to commemorate said service."

"Jumping the gun, isn't it?"

He laughs. "Seems Dickie's as eager to be done with the whole business as the rest of us. I think he sent them out a week ago. Though I have to credit his tenacity. He said August fifteenth from the time he agreed to partition, and we'll make it, after all."

I close the box and replace it on the table.

Father goes to the corner and lifts the lid on the giant trunk he had sent over by steamer almost a year ago. He lifts out various cases for the equipment and books and instruments.

He clears his throat once. Twice. "They want me to leave this afternoon, darling," he says, nestling a compass into its case.

I reel on him. "What?"

"We are to convene in Delhi tomorrow to finalize the maps with Governor Jenkins. The viceroy's staff fears such a gathering might present a perfect opportunity for those who might get up to mischief, so we've been asked to keep it a secret."

"But . . . but . . ." My mind races. Mischief? "But what about Mother? And me?"

"The evening papers tomorrow will carry word of the meeting. You'll likely be safer here without me. And you'll join me in Delhi on Friday, the day after the meeting. We might jog down to Agra and see the Taj Mahal before we head home. You'd like that, wouldn't you?"

I shrug. But the idea of the Taj doesn't have me excited. "Are you sure it'll be safe?"

"The Taj? I—"

I cut him off. "Not the Taj, Daddy. Us. You. Are we safe?"

He lays the box gently into the crate, walks over, and gives me a quick hug. "We'll be fine. They're just being cautious, is all."

I try to believe him, but it's hard. Hard now that the shine's worn off the whole Tariq thing. If he was plotting something, why not somebody else?

Daddy lets me go and returns to the packing. He picks up a scope and gives it a quick polish with his sleeve. "The Taj is wonderful, Meggie, you'll see." He rummages for the right case for the scope. "Now ring the girl for some tea, would you, please? And would you see if she has any more of that eggplant curry we had at lunch? And a few of the chapatis. They really are the most perfect little edible cutlery, aren't they? I'm going to hate going back to forks and things, but don't tell your mother."

"Certainly, Daddy," I say, reaching for the bell.

"I will miss those, I think," Father says, smiling to himself as he finds the correct case and buries the scope in the straw. "A sight better than a crumpet, I'd say."

I watch him for a moment more, wondering what else we'll miss, if I'll miss anything, before I turn and pull the cord for the bell that will bring Anu.

CHAPTER 20

TARIQ

The bell above the door at the telegraph office announces my departure as I walk slowly to my bicycle. I've just delivered what may well be the last of Mr. Darnsley's messages. A sort of dread is building slowly in my stomach. I don't have much time left to figure out how to get Margaret to help.

But I still can't bring myself to hurry back to the house. Instead, I turn for the lane leading home.

Half the houses on the street are empty. Squatters have taken up in some of them.

I roll to a stop in front of ours. The windows are shuttered; there's a lock on the gate. I put my foot down and catch myself as I remember my mother clinging to me, sobbing out her prayers for protection, Abbu's eyes on mine, asking me silently, *You see what you have done?*

The dread continues to well up inside me, choking off my breath, and I pump down on the pedals, racing away from that house and all I have given up. And for what? The slightest of hopes.

I ride hard, taking the ruts in the street with too much speed, glad to have each little impact rattle through the frame and into my bones, reminding me that I am still here. I stop at that same corner where I saw Sameer in the market that day I came home for lunch. But much has changed.

The block is ruined. The glass of the finer shops is shattered, the storefronts gaping like slack mouths, charred black by the fires that were set inside. A few pickers still comb the wreckage for bits of fabric from the cloth seller, or rice from the grocer, or medicine from the chemists. The bookshop I hid in is gone.

But two stalls remain relatively untouched.

The juti seller's.

And the goldsmith's.

The very ones I saw Sameer enter when I watched him that day a few weeks ago.

The crowd waiting to cross the lane surges forward, carrying me and the bicycle with them. I let the movement guide me across, drifting with it as I piece together what Sameer has been up to, how he came to have that gold chain that hung around his neck when I saw him last.

Sameer is extorting protection bribes from the merchants.

I'd heard Abbu complain about the bribes, how someone

would come into his shop promising to protect it if rioters came that way. He had no idea how it worked, and he refused to pay.

But others had. And Sameer had been collecting. Part of me can't help but admire him. It strikes me that had I thought about it sooner, I should have asked him how to handle Margaret and her father. He would have known what to do. More than that, Sameer would have known exactly *how* to do it.

Sameer wouldn't have moved too slowly with a girl like Margaret. Wouldn't have let his chance slip by.

The last time I saw him, he told me to be ready. What could he and his men need from me? Would they really help me if I did what they wanted? And what would it cost me? I guess it would be illegal, but how far a step could it be from how I've already tried to use the Darnsleys? How bad could it be?

Bad. Very bad.

No. Even if it meant getting me to Oxford, I couldn't do what Sameer asked me to do. The last time I went along with him, I may have killed someone. I wouldn't let it happen again.

Besides, Sameer's always been a liar. I could never trust him to make good on a promise. And he probably won't even live long enough to make it to Pakistan with all the risks he takes.

A liar. A liar taking too many risks.

Maybe I'm more like him than I want to admit.

The blasted bicycle chain slips off the crank again when I'm a hundred yards from the compound. It's the third time in two days. At least I'm close enough that I can wheel it back to the yellow house and fix it there.

I guide the wheel around a rickshaw wallah who offers to fix it for me if I give him a few paisa, past the bent man making roti on the corner in the tandoor. I'm hungry, realizing I missed lunch to get Darnsley's papers to the telegraph office. Maybe there's something left in the kitchen. My mind jumps just as quickly to wondering if Anu will still be in the kitchen.

Stop! I have to stop. I've got to make myself think of Margaret in the way that I cannot stop thinking of Anu. But I can't help it. Anu is already there in my mind, lingering, the image of her walking away, the way her braid rides against her neck, the way it sways as she walks . . .

Why can't it all go back to the way it was before? Back when Sikh was Sikh and Muslim was Muslim, but we were all Indian?

I cover half the distance to the house thinking of her, but then I see Sameer and freeze.

He's hanging back near the market on the opposite side of the margh. His two gundas, who follow him around like dogs, stand a ways off, the little one holding a parcel wrapped in brown paper. They're talking to a third man, a skinny wallah I recognize who does odd deliveries in the neighborhood. He is like me, running all over town, but with no regular employer. People call on him to get a meal carried to a sick friend, or a stack of books delivered from the booksellers when they don't want to carry them.

Sameer watches the three of them intently, one hand twisting the rope of gold at his neck.

I'm too far away to hear them, but the wallah tilts his head, screwing up his face in confusion, and points at the yellow walls of Darnsley's compound. One of the thugs reaches over and snaps his arm down, leans in close and whispers something, passing a roll of rupee notes into his palm. The wallah looks down at his hand, mouth falling open. But he still hesitates a moment before putting the money into his breast pocket and taking the parcel. He nods once. The others cross their arms and watch him walk away.

I begin to move again, let out the breath I didn't even know I was holding.

I have to stop that package.

I sprint across the road, passing the wallah and his parcel as I go. I avoid looking back at Sameer and his men. They can't know I've seen them. I push my bicycle through the gap the porter opens for me. I'm close enough to hear Margaret's harmonium now, so I glance up quickly. This time she is not watching me.

The wallah, avoiding looking either me or the guard in the eye, holds out the parcel to the guard. He takes it, and the wallah runs off.

"Who's it for?" I ask the guard in Punjabi.

The man studies the label and screws up his face, the wrinkles in his brow matching the ones in his turban. "The mister."

This is bad. Very bad. Dread opens up a hole in my gut, sucking everything in. "I'll take it," I say, perhaps too quickly.

The guard shrugs, hands me the box. It's heavier than I expected. I lay it carefully in my basket and head for the back of the house. I shouldn't look back, but I can't help it.

Standing across the lane, perfectly still as the crowds stream back and forth around him, is Sameer. And he is staring at me.

I trip over the bike, almost fall, almost dump the package from the basket.

Sameer just stares, his jaw twitching, eyes flashing.

The guard misses all of this. "Hurry!" he shouts. "Darnsley goes." He points at the great black car idling in front of the house, waiting to carry Mr. Darnsley away.

I make a face at him, not sure I heard him right. "Now?"

"Haan," he barks, gesturing up toward the study windows. "Waiting for you." He sounds disgusted to admit this last part, but I'm too scared to be insulted. I have to get rid of the box. But I have to get upstairs. It is my last chance. Maybe he has changed his mind.

I run the bike across the yard, and can feel Sameer still staring at me as I go. Once I reach the back of the house, I move quickly, leaning my bicycle up against the wall, and then unlatching the small door in the rear wall that leads to the alley.

I don't want to leave it here, but it will have to do. I can't risk missing Mr. Darnsley. I'll take it to the river as soon as he goes. I glance around me to make sure no one is watching, then I gingerly lift the package from the basket, careful not to jostle whatever is lying inside. It could be a cobra, like the one sent to Radcliffe in Delhi. I lower it onto the rubbish pile, pulling some loose paper over its sides until it is hidden. I straighten, scan the alley, and realize with a start that I cannot hear Margaret playing anymore. I look up to the back windows in the library, hoping she has not followed me here. Blessedly, the windows are empty. Taking a deep breath, I slip back inside the door and bolt through the kitchen.

Anu is not here, but the old woman looks up from the pan of aloo gobi she is stirring on the burner. She mutters to herself in Bengali, cursing me, and returns to the potatoes. I'm used to her disapproval. But now her curses feel somehow earned.

I pass through, grabbing an apple and a handful of cold naan when she is not looking. My fingers brush up against the scabbard of the knife tied at my hip when I shove the apple into my pyjamas. I'm folding one of the pieces of naan and cramming it whole into my mouth when a voice surprises me. "What are you doing?" Margaret is at the top of the stair, looking down. Dust swims in the air between us.

I almost choke on the plug of bread in my mouth when I try to speak.

"Where have you been?" she asks sharply.

I swallow, attempt a smile but can't with all the food in my mouth. I keep my lips sealed. Grimace. Nod.

She descends a few steps as she keeps her eyes locked on

mine. But it's not like before. There is nothing longing or moony about her now. The fire has moved from her cheeks into her eyes. Her chin tilts up so that she looks down the length of her nose at me.

"You were quite long in returning from the telegraph office," she accuses. And I begin to understand that she is angry with me. Furious, even.

"The b-bicycle," I stammer, "the chain—"

"And pinching food from the kitchen, I see," she says, nodding at the bread still in my hand. I look at it as I try to force down the bite in my mouth. And I realize that maybe I should not worry about my plans surviving, but my own survival instead.

"I missed the meal when I—"

"Don't let it happen again," she says dismissively. "Father wants to see you. He leaves in moments. But he has been waiting for you. After he goes, there are trunks to pack. I think he means to send some as early as the morning."

"Tomorrow?" I say, realizing that if their things are going, she will not be far behind.

Margaret nods. "There's nothing left for us to do here." She pauses, takes another step closer. She's almost as tall as I am. I'd nearly forgotten.

She waits a moment after that last word before sliding past me for the front door. I watch her go, my last desperate, stupid hope trailing in her wake.

I stand there in the dim hall a moment, the bread soggy now

against my palm, and wonder how I will find Abbu and Ammi in Pakistan. How I will face them, if I can find them at all.

I shove the naan into my pyjamas with the apple. My appetite is gone. The stairs seem steeper than they did this morning as I climb them. And stupidly, I still wonder where Anu is.

I find Mr. Darnsley in the study where I left him, wrapping the stand for the transit in a piece of velvet.

"Finally," he says without looking up. "I was beginning to worry."

"Sorry," I say. Why is Margaret so angry with me? What did I do wrong? Just an hour or two ago, we were talking. Did she hate the chocolate?

Mr. Darnsley interrupts my thoughts. "Are you all right, Tariq?"

I gulp, searching for words. "The young miss said you are leaving," I manage lamely.

He leans against the corner of his desk. "The car is waiting downstairs."

"Shall I continue packing these for you?"

"In the crate there," he says, pointing at the box stationed on the floor. I open the door of the bookcase and begin pulling down the volumes and wedging them into the box. Filling up every inch of space by puzzling the books against one another.

"What do you think will happen, Tariq?" he asks me, acting like he isn't in a rush, like there is not a giant car waiting downstairs to drive him away from this place forever.

Startled by the question, I look up. "Sir?"

He is staring at one of the few maps remaining unpacked. "Mountbatten secured promises from all sides back in June that whatever the boundary looked like, no one would raise a fuss about it."

I had read as much in the papers.

"Do you think they will keep their word?" he asked.

The stack of books I'm holding grows heavy. Why does he care what I think? "It is difficult to say, sir."

He sighs. We both know it's going to get worse. He changes the subject.

"You've been a model employee."

"Thank you, sir," I say. The box is nearly half-full now.

"I've taken the liberty of writing you a reference," he says, reaching for an envelope. "When you arrive in Pakistan, I hope it will prove useful to have some testimonial from a former employer. When you apply at university, for instance."

I stare at the simple brown envelope in his hand, the same shade as the paper on the parcel I just buried in the rubbish heap. I almost laugh at it. At the gesture. I should be grateful for the kindness. I should be thankful for his concern. I should be content to have taken my place in a long line of my forebears who have served dutifully at the right hand of the British Raj.

I should.

I hesitate. What if I delivered Sameer's package? If Darnsley can cast me off, if Margaret can throw me over, and all I've got to show for all my work and sacrifice is one budhoo letter, then what do I owe them?

But I take the letter, mutter my thanks, and lay it on the table next to where I'm working.

"You'll be running Pakistan in no time," he says, shaking my hand, collecting his briefcase, and stalking out the door.

Running. I'll be running, I think as I hear his footfalls on the stairs.

I stand there for a while, hating him for the fact that he will return to England. He gets to go. Just like that.

And I'm trapped here.

Outside, I hear Mrs. Darnsley and Margaret shouting their good-byes as the car drives away.

It is over, I realize. He has gone. I'm finished. My bitterness grows as I clean up after him, pack his supplies, his maps. I envy every single piece I place inside every box, because they're going where I never will.

CHAPTER 21

ANUPREET

"I miss him already," Margaret sighs, looking out the window.

"It's barely been an hour," her mother points out. "And the sooner we get these things packed, the sooner we can join him." She picks up the wooden box where she stores her jewelry, carries it to the bed, and settles herself on the cover. "Go on, then," she says to Margaret gently.

Margaret doesn't move. "How long do you think it will take my harmonium to get to London?" she asks, catching my eye. I see the mischief in her look and have to dig my fingernail into my palm to keep from laughing.

Mrs. Darnsley sets her jaw. "There will be no need for that thing in London," she says. "You'll have your piano."

Margaret keeps her expression solemn—how does she do that? She is, to borrow my favorite of her phrases, winding up her mother. "I'm quite sotted with it, though. Glenn Miller sounds divine on it, and Beethoven's not bad, either."

"Margaret—"

"Really, Mummy, I could play it for your ladies' circle. Won't it be a treat? A nice, musical way to remind everyone of all the important work we've been doing abroad—"

"Go and pack, darling," Mrs. Darnsley says, smirking. "You can open up a music school when we get back for all I care, so long as we're home."

Margaret rolls her eyes, annoyed her mother won't play along. "Fine," she says, backing into the hall. "But I'm dead serious about humping it home with us."

"You sound like a common soldier," her mother scolds without looking up from her earrings and necklaces. "Honestly."

Margaret smiles at me, sticks her tongue out at her mother as she clicks her heels together, throws a hand up in salute, and marches off to her room.

I've been helping the ladies pack since this morning. I knew something was coming, but it wasn't until the car was readied that I realized Mr. Darnsley was leaving. Old Shibani in the kitchen told me it was meant to be a secret, meant to keep the family safer if their comings and goings weren't known.

But since then I've been too busy packing up their wardrobes to give much thought to what they need to be kept safe from.

And I'm glad to be busy. When my hands fall still, my mind is given to conjuring up pictures of the insides of train cars . . . of imagining whether my tiny cousins—the little ones who weren't even old enough yet to go to school—were killed quickly on the train with the rest, or taken, sold, and hurt. It turns my stomach to pray that they are dead, that they are not suffering, but I pray it daily.

Mrs. Darnsley sits on her bed, carefully wrapping up her earrings and combs in small cotton squares, then tucking them into a velvet roll. "I can't say I'm sorry to be leaving India," she says to me. "It never did grow on me as they say it does."

It stings to hear her say this. And I wish I had enough words in English to make her understand that she hasn't seen the real India. Not the one I know. This version of my home has more in common with a python shedding its skin. Ugly. Messy. Mean.

This isn't India! I want to scream at her. But it wouldn't do any good. She's already made up her mind.

So I say nothing, folding up a dress I've never seen Mrs. Darnsley wear, taking care not to flatten the little ruffles lined up on either side of the buttons. So many clothes, all in wonderful fabrics. Soft cottons and wool so light and smooth I wonder at what the sheep must be like in England. But the colors are sad whites, muted grays, and tans. Strange that a fine lady as wealthy as Mrs. Darnsley seems so afraid of color. And I imagine the garments made over in proper crimsons, purples, and golds.

I smile as I fold them over themselves carefully, sliding paper so thin between the folds as my mistress has shown me. To prevent wrinkles, she told me.

"When you've finished mine, you can help Margaret," she says, tucking another bundle into the case. "Though that girl has probably simply crammed everything into her trunks. I think she's even more eager to leave than I am."

She can't be, I think. Not like her mother. She'll miss me; I know it. Won't she?

And what will happen to me when they've gone? Maybe Papaji and Biji will let me go back to school, let me out of the house again since nothing bad has happened to me while I've been here.

"I don't know when we'll—" Mrs. Darnsley begins before a sound like thunder cuts her short.

For a split second my heart lifts at the prospect of rain, of the real monsoon arriving, of a single clap of thunder followed by a flood of water from the heavens.

But thunder doesn't shatter glass.

The windows on the south wall of the room, the ones over-looking the top of the rear wall and the small alley, shatter, the glass dripping inward like the rain I'd almost expected. The mirror on the small vanity table cracks from top to bottom, and the tiny vials and pots of lotions that Mrs. Darnsley uses on her face skitter across the polished surface. One near the edge leaps to the floor, the scent of jasmine flooding the room along with something else.

Smoke and dust and plaster.

And then Mrs. Darnsley is screaming.

Her screams come like an echo, filling the room with noise and fear and surprise. I can't seem to remember how to move, my bare feet planted in a sea of broken glass. I stare at the floor, waiting to see if my blood appears there in fat drops as it did that afternoon in the shop those months ago.

I realize that perhaps this is the only reason I know it is a bomb, the only reason I'm not screaming as Mrs. Darnsley is. Somehow my mind recalled the sound of a bomb from that day.

When no blood appears on the floor, I toss the blouse back into the wardrobe, and then pick my way across the floor to the bed where my mistress sits shaking on the cover.

"Ma'am!" I say.

She looks to me, eyes wide, cheeks flushed, hands shaking around a pearl necklace she had been in the middle of stowing when the blast came. She screams again.

I place a hand on her shoulder. "Are you hurt?"

"Margaret!" she barks after a silence. I hurry across for the door, picking up a sliver of glass in my toe as I go, Mrs. Darnsley following close behind. We bolt across the hall to Margaret's room.

She's sitting on the floor, whiter than I ever thought she could get, given how pale she is to start with. All her windows are intact. "Was that—?" Margaret asks, looking at her mother.

Her mother nods, scoops her up in her arms. Hugs her fiercely. "I think so. It certainly sounded like a bomb."

I turn, run back across the hall in the direction of where the sound came from. Margaret and her mother are right behind me.

The little sitting room is showered in glass. We tiptoe across the bits, cluster at one shattered window, and look out into the back alley.

So much dust still shimmers in the air; I choke with the thickness of it. Through the haze, I see a great chunk of the wall missing. Beyond this hole, the rubbish pile is strewn all over the street. A few stragglers are still running from the site, toward the lines of people crowding either end of the alley, looking to see what caused the noise, if anyone is hurt.

But only one person is running *toward* the place where the bomb went off.

Tariq.

He rounds the corner of the compound, pushing through the throng and breaking into the alley. He runs toward the hole in the wall, eyes wild. When he reaches it, when he sees, he stops, leans over, clutching at his stomach as if he will be sick. Then he stands, pushes his hair back from his forehead like he's trying to pull it out, and looks around. He scans the crowds gathered at either side, like he's looking for someone.

Then his face pales even more, and I follow his eyes to the pile of clothing near the hole in the wall.

It stirs. A flash of green . . . a green kurta. The little boy!

Tariq is running to him—the boy who has been picking about in the rubbish heap since the Darnsleys came to stay.

The boy Margaret's been leaving presents for back there since that day her father and Tariq came back from the north. Nahi! Nahi!

"God in heaven . . . ," Margaret whispers, grabbing my arm, seeing what I am seeing.

Tariq scoops the boy into his arms, just in time to hand him to the wailing woman who has appeared in the clearing. The boy's mother. The child makes no sound, as if he is sleeping, though his leg is a bloody mess.

"Oh, God," Margaret wails, making as if she means to run to the stairs and out to the alley.

"Stop!" her mother screams, catching her with surprising speed, holding her fast with even more surprising strength. "Stop!" she repeats, eyes flashing as she forces her daughter to look at her. "There might be another blast! You can't go out there!"

Margaret tries to wrestle away, but who knew how strong her mother was? After a moment Margaret slumps against her. "But the little boy—" She breaks off with a sob.

The sound of the boy's mother screaming, crying for a doctor, pulls me back to the window. She and the boy are almost out of my sight, but Tariq stands frozen there, looking wildly around. Like he's searching for someone in particular.

What is he doing?

And then Tariq seems to ask himself the same question. He backs up quickly, hurries back toward the crowd, the crowd that's already thinning out. He dives into the mass, pushes his way back through, upsetting a man carrying spools of mattress webbing on his head. The coils tumble free, but Tariq doesn't stop, doesn't even slow down as he hurries back to the front of the house and out of sight.

"You saw no one in the alley before?" the sipahi asks me.

"Nahi," I tell the policemen. I'm almost sure this one has already asked me his questions. The same questions. They all ask me the same questions. All of us.

I do not understand.

I do not understand how one bomb that goes off in an alley behind this house raises such a fuss.

There are fires and terrifying noises every night now. Markets sacked. Temples burned. Whole trains of people murdered.

And no one asks questions about any of those.

None of the officers ask about the child, either. And none can answer my questions about his well-being, even though I persist in asking, tell them repeatedly that my mistress wishes to know how he is.

They are not concerned for one beggar boy.

But there are more policemen here now than I've ever seen in one place. Their brown uniforms and polished clubs litter the courtyard, fanning around the gates and the street outside the Darnsleys' home like a small army.

And the right hand doesn't seem to know what the left

is doing. They all chase one another around, getting in one another's way, ask us the same questions over and over again, making a show of how important a matter this is to the police.

Because apparently it's the closest anyone's come to killing one of the men working on the boundary award.

The officer questioning me now pushes at his pagri, edging back the band, the fine hair at his temple stuck to his skin by sweat.

He looks at me. They all look at me. They pretend to want to know what I might have seen. But then they all ask the question eventually.

He points at my scar. "How did that happen?"

"I was in a shop. A window broke. The glass," I say.

He shakes his head as if it is merely an inconvenience. "Pity."

I start to move back into the house, back to a bit of work before another of the inspectors can intercept me. But this one is persistent.

"You saw nothing, then?" he asks.

I hesitate. What did I see? What made Tariq run toward the blast?

I shake my head. "Nahi."

He lets me go.

Inside the house, I hurry back up the stairs to Mrs. Darnsley's room. Shibani and I have already swept up all the broken glass. And now Ma'am is even more eager to finish packing, finish leaving.

"Good, Anu," she says when I return. She is warmer toward me now. I don't know if it has to do with what we've been through, or if it's because of the stuff she's been drinking since we all came back inside. The dozens of little pots and vials on her dressing table have been packed away, replaced by only one bottle of amber-colored liquid. It's half-empty now.

I resume my work at her wardrobe. After folding three dresses and boxing up a hat I've never seen her wear, she lights a cigarette and speaks again.

"We had bombs in London, you know," she says, pulling at the cigarette, "during the war."

"Yes, ma'am," I say.

"Awful time," she says. "Blackout curtains, the sirens . . ."

I do not know what blackout curtains are.

"But it seems there was always warning. We always knew when they were coming, even if it was only a few minutes."

I continue packing.

"This feels different. So unexpected. So surprising. It's almost . . . unseemly."

"Bombs are rarely seemly, Mother," Margaret says, appearing in the doorway.

"You know what I mean," she says.

"Have they told you anything?" Margaret asks, leaning against the wardrobe. "The policemen? I want to know who did this! I want to know who the bastards are who tried to kill Daddy, who hurt that little boy—" She cuts herself off, angry tears welling in her eyes. She wipes them quickly away with the back of her hand.

"Darling—" Her mother pats the cover on the bed, inviting Margaret to sit. But Margaret shakes her head.

Mrs. Darnsley rises from the bed and moves toward her daughter. "You've had a shock, Margaret."

"We've all had a shock!" Margaret cries. "And that poor boy has had his leg all botched to pieces if he's even still alive and I want to know who . . ." She crosses her arms, stares at the ceiling, unable to finish. I stare at my hands, wish there was more I could do. Wish there was some reassurance I could give them.

"My Margaret." Mrs. Darnsley strokes her daughter's hair. "Always such fire. Anu, did you know that most of the children were removed from London during the worst of the bombing? Thousands of them carted away on trains to live in country homes. We almost sent Meggie, but she was just old enough to remain. And she was so brave. Insisted on staying, didn't you, poppet?"

Margaret doesn't seem to be listening. "When do we go?" she asks in defeat, her face buried in her mother's shoulder, voice muffled. She is done being brave now.

"She wanted to do her bit," Mrs. Darnsley says to me. "There were loads of things girls did. Meggie volunteered with the Red Cross, isn't that right?"

"Father must be halfway to Delhi by now," Margaret says instead of answering, drawing back from her mother, wiping her nose. I feel out of place here, listening to them talk around each other. It seems too private somehow.

"Of course she met that man and, well, we all know how that turned out," Mrs. Darnsley says. "And then we ended up here."

Margaret goes still, closes her eyes, and then opens them. And she is different now, like one of the vanara from the Rama stories who can change their shapes at will. "Well done, Mother. It only took you a few hours to blame a bombing here in the Punjab on my indiscretions in London."

But Mrs. Darnsley doesn't want to fight. She simply reaches back out and pulls her daughter in, wrapping her in a slow embrace, the cigarette still in her fingers. Margaret's eyes lock on mine, the wisp of smoke curls up from behind her.

She looks away first.

"We go tomorrow," her mother says finally. "When Daddy arrives in Delhi this evening and hears what has happened, he'll send the car straight back for us. We'll make for Delhi as soon as it returns. Once there, we'll hop on the first aeroplane we can."

"We won't have to stay longer while they sort out who did this?" Margaret asks, pushing away.

Mrs. Darnsley shakes her head and crosses to the dressing table. She refills the glass and drinks it down at a gulp.

"How much have you had?" Margaret asks.

Her mother doesn't answer, just smiles, crosses back to her daughter, and adjusts one of her curls.

Margaret turns to me, as if I am somehow responsible. "How much has she had?"

This time I look away.

She gives up, asks her first question again: "We don't have to stay until the police find out who left the bomb?"

Her mother sounds sleepy. "That might take ages. And if we stay longer, they may try again."

"Then why don't we go tonight?" Margaret asks quickly. "Isn't there an overnight train to Delhi?"

Her mother hesitates and seems to look sideways at me before speaking. "The trains have shut down," she says.

I flinch, pictures I don't want to see flashing into my mind. The trains. My cousins. My uncle and auntie.

"How does the whole bleeding railway shut down?" Margaret asks.

My legs won't hold me up, turning into kheer. I grab the bedpost to steady myself. *Bleeding.* I've always managed to somehow only picture Papaji's brother and family as sort of quietly dead. Sleeping almost. But there would have been blood. So much of it. Everywhere.

Mrs. Darnsley is looking at me, curious, concerned. She knows. But how? Papaji told the guard when he brought me back that day. But how did it work its way back to her? "There were troubles with some of the trains. Some attacks by the highwaymen or—"

"Dacoits," I say, just so she'll think I'm all right. We call train robbers dacoits. At least we used to when they were just little bands of desperate men looking to line their pockets, not great mobs of Muslim men looking to attack trains full of Sikhs and Hindus coming out of the north, or mobs of Sikh men attacking Muslim trains going the other way. Dacoit seems too simple a word now for what they are.

"Thank you, Anu," Mrs. Darnsley says softly. She looks sorry to have to talk about all this. But Margaret doesn't seem to notice.

"Can't we round up another car?"

"Not on such short notice. Besides, the police captain promised he'd supply a dozen extra guards until we've gone. Whoever it was won't try anything with so many policemen about."

"How can he be sure?"

She shrugs. "We can't. But we're safer in here for now. Whoever left that bomb couldn't even get it inside the compound. We're lucky."

And I think to myself that they are. They are able to leave this place, go back to London, where safety and home await them, while the rest of us remain here, trying to dig both out of the rubble.

CHAPTER 22

MARGARET

I've given up asking after the little boy, but I can't stop thinking about him. Can't stop thinking about what I did.

Anu didn't know his name, and I've seen almost nothing of Tariq since he carried the poor child to his mother, but I doubt he knows him either. None of the officers seem to even care. But I can hardly stand it—I need to know. If only I had listened to Father, if only I hadn't been leaving gifts for him, then he might not have been the one to find the bomb. Even Anu told me not to do it, but did I listen? Fool! A little boy, just a little boy, is hurt, and it's in part, yes, it is, my fault. Fool!

Even when I try to do something good, it all goes pear shaped. First Alec. Now the little boy. And I can't find a way to make up for it.

Below stairs, the policemen still loiter in the halls and rooms, still inventing reasons to question Mother, the servants, me.

They're all over the courtyard. Some question the porters and staff, while others check every nook and cranny of the compound for other hidden explosives. I wonder absently if they'll find my cigarette stash.

It's queer, this feeling. Nothing at all like the bombs in London going off. Those were dropped from airplanes, falling from thousands of feet in areas Jerry guessed would do the most damage. They likely had little notion of the people the bombs fell on, the gardens or churches or homes they destroyed that were near enough to the factories or other spots that were their intended targets.

But this bomb, though it was small, though it only blasted through a wall and broke some glass in the back windows of a house that will sit empty again in a day's time, is strangely more frightening. It was deliberate. Someone wanted to *kill* Father. Or us. And maybe they merely wanted to sink a knife in the back of the empire as we packed up and hurried away from the Crown Jewel, but all the same, it was left at *our* house.

I slip into the little parlor. Anu and Shibani have already cleaned up all the broken glass off the floor. I stand at the back window, now just a jagged hole without the panes in place, and look down at the spot where the bomb went off. Odd they'd choose the rear of the compound, and our trash heap, to teach us a lesson. All the same, I'm grateful they weren't any bolder.

I pull away from the window and go back to my room. I'll make myself barmy staring at the spot, thinking of that poor little boy. . . .

I have to keep busy, so I take up again with packing my things.

My wardrobe is nearly done, and I've asked Anu to see if she can send someone out to find a crate to ship my harmonium in. I start gathering up the bottles on my dressing table when I see Tariq framed in the mirror behind me.

He's jumpy, hands pulling at the hem of his kurta, usually pressed to perfection. He's not nervous and sweet like before, but panicked. *Good,* I think, *let the tosser stew a bit.*

"What?" I ask without turning round.

He hesitates, glances into the hall before stepping into the room. "Your mother sent me to see if you have any baggage for me to carry below stairs yet."

I look now, examining his reflection. He's still handsome, but this strange jitteriness that seems to have settled on him highlights his faults somehow. His cheeks are marked with spotty little scars, a telling reminder that he may have once been more awkward and ungainly than he is now. The underarms of his shirt are dark with perspiration; one of his front teeth has a corner chipped away. I wonder that I didn't see it before.

His accent is back in force, like he can't hold it in the way he has the last couple of months. And his words aren't as smooth as they once seemed to my ear, his voice rising and cracking halfway through his announcement. And they don't ring true, either.

"Mother knows I haven't finished packing anything," I say, twisting on the stool to face him, folding my arms across my chest.

He opens his mouth as if he will say more, but stops. He takes another step into the room, craning his neck to get a look out my window. "She—" he begins before I cut him short.

"You're lying," I say to him, enjoying at last the feeling of my own strength, of being rid of the spell of him.

He forgets to argue as he stares out the window at the street. I follow his eye to the space beyond the wall, the corner of the lane across from the compound.

"What do you want?" I ask him, even enjoying the fact that I feel annoyed by his presence, annoyed by his odd behavior, his anxiety. I reckon it means I am truly free of him.

"You can see from here," he says to himself, skin going grey like cold ashes from the end of a cigarette.

I don't know what he's talking about, but I'm relishing how the tables have turned. After nearly two months of finding myself the uncertain schoolgirl where he's been concerned, I like feeling that for once I have the upper hand.

"Of course I can," I say. "My father gave me the room with the best view."

He points at the harmonium in front of the window, still waiting to be packed. "You sit here and play. But you watch me," he says, looking at me now, accusing.

I straighten my shoulders. "There is damned little else to watch for," I say, adding quickly, "take care not to flatter yourself. I've seen better."

He doesn't seem to be really hearing me. "But now you will not look at me. Now you seem to hate the sight of me." He's not asking a question. More that he's piecing something together—only, I don't know what it is. Like when I used to sit at Mother's feet on the floor as she did her needlework. From my point of view, what was inside the hoop was a tangle of knots and crossed threads, but when she'd turn it to show me, the picture of a bluebird on a nest was neat and clean and perfect.

Only, now I'm annoyed enough at not knowing what he's driving at to pretend that I do. And maybe I do. Maybe he understands what I know of his kindness toward me running parallel with his desperation to reach England.

"And why wouldn't I, after what you've tried to pull?" I say sharply.

His eyes widen with terror. "You know?"

"Of course I know!" I spit, springing up from the stool and clearing some ground between us. He's too close all of a sudden. "Do you think I'm a total duffer?"

He's too panicked to realize he should tell me otherwise.

"You must help me," he begs, taking a step forward.

I back away sharply. "Help you? After what you've done? You're barmy!"

"But you *know*," he begs, taking another careful step toward me. "You know I didn't mean to. It was all a terrible coincidence... you must understand—"

"Understand?" I say, realizing the word shot free with more emotion than I wanted to show him. More than he deserved. I look to the door to make sure Mother hasn't heard, isn't coming to investigate.

"Are you quite finished?" I ask him, lowering my voice. But now he looks at me as quizzically as I did him a moment ago.

"But you told no one. . . ." He drifts off, confused.

I hesitate. Are we talking about the same thing?

"You could have told the police," he goes on.

I laugh. "Tell them what? That you've been pretending to fancy me so you might woo your way to London? Sorry to disappoint, but I'm not so easy you can have me for some old poems or a pack of smokes and a lousy nib of chocolate!"

He slumps against the window, lets loose a stream of Punjabi, eyes shut tight against my words, my face, my existence. I do not know what he says, but I hear the word *Allah* repeated often enough to think he might be praying. And I wonder, *Is he asking for forgiveness?* And shouldn't he be asking me?

"Sod off," I whisper, turning away from him to find Mother standing in the hall outside my room. Her eyes settle on mine, fix there and study me. It's the same stare she gave me when she first learned of Alec. And I know she's heard. Maybe not every word, but the important bits at least.

"What my daughter means, young man, is that it is most definitely time for you to get back to work," Mother says, taking a step into the room. Her appearance pulls Tariq up and away from the window, his mutterings ending in something like a sob. His eyes widen as she draws nearer. But in spite of his fear, his gaze snaps back to me, and I see that he has not finished asking me questions. Is not finished trying to suss out what I might have seen from my window.

Why does he care what I saw? After what he's tried to pull on me? After someone has tried to kill Daddy? Has hurt or killed that little boy?

"Go and help Anupreet clean up the mess behind the compound." Mother sways a little on her feet, but her voice is steely, removed, in the way that she sometimes speaks to servants at home who suffer the misfortune of irritating her. As if she will not dignify them by imbuing them with emotion of any sort. "Now," she adds, listing a bit with the command. I wonder how far into the bottle she's gotten.

Tariq takes a breath, bows his head, and scurries for the door. Mother is still standing just inside the room, her eyes finding mine now. But she doesn't move, instead forcing upon Tariq the humiliation of pressing himself against the wall and edging out the door behind her.

We listen as his footsteps echo down the stairs, followed by the sound of the door off the kitchen creaking open, the slam of it shutting. I wonder if he'll crawl through the hole to attend to Mother's orders, or if he'll run around to the front of the house and use the gate. And I hate that part of me still wants to hurry to the back windows to see if I can see him there. But Mother's words bring me back to myself.

"Up to your old tricks again, Margaret?" she asks, tone unchanged from her orders for Tariq. And it's a credit to her strength that I can't think of a single thing to say back.

CHAPTER 23

TARIQ

She doesn't know.

At least not yet. I can't believe it. Can't believe she didn't see me bring the package into the compound, take it behind the house. She doesn't know.

Not that it matters much. I'm finished.

Even if no one ever finds out that I brought the bomb inside, even if they believe me that I didn't know what it was, it's still over. All of it.

My grandfather would tell me not to give up, I suppose. But Abbu was right. Daadaa was old. He was a dreamer.

But I'm a chutiyaa. I've been such an idiot, thinking I could make this all work to my advantage. And now I'm stuck here. Alone.

All that's left for me to do is to try to find my family. I haven't heard from them since they left. And the trains haven't been running since the massacre near Amritsar. I'll have to go on foot.

I don't want to wait, but I can't run now; the police already suspect me. If I bolt, they'll have all the reasons they need to blame me. And there's no guarantee they won't find me before I cross the border.

No. I'll wait. As soon as the Darnsleys leave Jalandhar and the police give up on finding the bomber, I'll go. Not even the porter knows that the package I collected from him was the bomb that blew up the back wall. No one knows except Sameer, and I can avoid him until I leave.

I just have to hang on a bit longer. Survive.

For the moment that means obeying Mrs. Darnsley. So I head for the alley to clean up the mess.

The back gate is already boarded over, the portion of the wall that held it destroyed by the blast. I go to the front, where I run the gauntlet of policemen, who glare at me, sure I had some part in this because I am Muslim. Allah knows I look guilty enough for it, but they've asked me their questions and seemed fine with my answers. For now. But I know. They're Sikh, most of them, and eager for a scapegoat.

Maybe I should tell them about Sameer. No. They'll never believe I didn't have something more to do with it. Even if they caught him, Sameer would probably manage to convince them that it was my idea. And that's if they caught him. He's too smart to let himself get caught. Not like me.

Stupid, stupid me.

I run past the policemen to the side lane to reach the rear of the compound.

Dusky light from the other side filters through the planks over the jagged hole in the wall. Anu squats low in the gathering shadows, sorting the debris into two bins.

She speaks without looking up. She's seemed afraid of me since that afternoon in the kitchen. "Patthar." She points at the pail as a small stone clangs into the bucket, and then to a pile at the base of the wall, readied there for when the proper repairs will be done. The other bin contains the muck and trash of the household.

I nod, join her on the ground, and start sorting. I steal glances at her from time to time. Even with her hands caked in dust and grease, even with the sweat standing on her forehead, she is beautiful. Beautiful as she cleans up after someone else's mess. My mess.

Suddenly I want to tell her that I tried to stop it, that had I known it was an actual bomb instead of just a snake, like I thought, then I would never have left it for later. Would she believe me? Would she believe that I had no idea anybody would be hurt?

I glance around. Only hours ago there were crowds three people deep on either side of the alley, but now no one. We're alone. I could tell her. Right now. I could tell her that it was all a terrible accident, that I didn't do anything wrong. Somehow, if she would believe me, I could get through this.

But I don't get a chance to find out. For rounding the south corner of the compound is Sameer. And following behind him, his two gundas.

"No, no, no," I whisper, before I catch myself.

Anu looks sharply at me, confused.

Why now? Why in front of her?

Before she can ask a thing, I stand, run to intercept Sameer.

Sameer gives me a look of disgust, then points at the wall. "Not what I had in mind," he says to me.

I clench the stone I'd been about to deposit in the pail hard in my fist. "You shouldn't be here."

He steps forward, jabs my chest with his finger. "No," he seethes, "it is you who should not have been *there*." He points toward the front of the house. "You took the parcel—"

"I always carry deliveries for Mr. Darnsley—"

He puts an arm around my shoulders, ignoring my excuse, steering me around to face the damage of the blast squarely. "You know how hard it is to get explosives? How expensive?"

"Sameer—"

"What will I tell the men who organized this? How would you explain to them that the bomb they so carefully built was wasted on a useless stone wall, behind the house, no less. . . ."

He's so calm. I think it scares me more than if he were yelling and punching me. But he's so in control, with his arm across my shoulders, his words like he's some sort of schoolmaster chastising the stupid schoolboy.

How could I not have seen how dangerous he was before?

"I didn't know it was a bomb," I whisper.

He lifts his eyebrows. "Really? Would we send flowers to the good Mr. Darnsley for a job well done? Is that what you believed?"

"N-no . . . ," I stammer. "I thought—"

"Ahh," he says coldly. "You thought?" He clamps his arm down tighter across my shoulders and digs his thumb into the muscle. "That is a problem, friend. Tariq, always thinking, always first in the class. But this was not something for you to think about."

"Someone could have been killed," I say, knowing it is stupid to point this out to Sameer, who wanted someone killed, but I don't know what else to say. "There was a beggar boy who nearly was—"

"A beggar?" he asks, disgusted. "The bomb was built to go off when the box was opened. Tell me how the package I had delivered came to find itself in the hands of a beggar boy?"

"I—"

"All you had to do was give it to him," he fumes, "and you shouldn't have even had that much to do. I suspected you had no stomach to go with all those brains. You impressed me that day at the gurdwara, the way you dropped that Sikh. But maybe that was a rare lapse of courage for you."

I feel—truly *feel*—the blood drain from my face as I force myself not to look at Anu, pray that she doesn't understand what Sameer has just said. I could handle almost anyone else knowing, just not her.

"We thought at first to have you deliver it, but we used the wallah instead. Let us just say we were worried we could not count on you. And we were right, weren't we, you interfering ghadda."

"You should go," I say, trying another tack. Anything to get him to leave. "Someone might hear you. The policemen are still out in front." But they are too far to hear us, and there is no one around to fetch them. No one but Anu, who crouches frozen, a few yards away.

He laughs. "You are concerned for my safety now? How loyal—"

He stops abruptly as I see Anu rise and begin to run. "Grab her!" he barks at his two friends. They move quicker than I thought possible, overtaking her before she can reach the corner of the house.

And suddenly the nightmare gets worse.

"Did you hear something that upset you, girl?" Sameer asks as he pulls me over to her.

Anu is struggling against the bigger of the two men. He has one hand over her mouth, his other arm locked around her chest, pinning her arms to her sides. The other gunda stands a few steps behind, smirking, checking over his shoulder every few seconds to make sure that no one is coming.

Sameer seems to have forgotten how furious he is with me

as he examines Anu. "And who is this, Tariq?" he asks, reaching for the end of her braid, lifting it and letting it fall back down from his fingers. The beads she keeps woven there rattle against one another.

"Let her go," I say, hating how weak I sound. "She's just a rag picker. I've never seen her before." The lie is a good one. Nearly all the garbage that comes from the house is sifted through by beggars and paupers, some collecting bits of fabric or paper or anything else that can be used or sold. "She doesn't know anything."

Sameer chuckles, shakes his head. "Oh, Tariq," he says, tracing Anu's nose with one finger. He can't touch her. Not her! My hand goes to my hip, hovering over the hidden knife. I can't let him—

"You lie to me now. Before you only interfered, but now you lie?" He wags a finger at me as though this disappointment is somehow more serious than the bomb. "She works in the house with you. I was only asking for her name."

How am I so stupid? Of course they recognize her. They've been watching me, so they'd have seen her at some point as well. I'm a greater fool than Sameer says I am.

"I followed her once, a couple of months ago," he says, "but she was with some tall haramzada. They lost us in the market. But"—his eyes cut toward Anu—"I've often dreamed what might have happened had we caught her."

I can tell by the way Anu's eyes widen and her feet stop

kicking for a moment that Sameer is telling the truth. A new wave of panic rises in me.

"Let her go," I plead.

Sameer laughs now. "Surely you've finished with her by now, haven't you?" He's challenging me. The way he used to dare me to throw a stone at the window of the gurdwara.

I know what he means, and fury burns inside me to hear him talk about her that way. But I'm ashamed, too. Ashamed at the thoughts *I've* had about Anu. I let my silence answer for me.

"I see," he says, almost cordially. "Best not to soil your own bed. Right, my friend?"

I want to shout that I am not his friend. That I am nothing like him. But instead I just say, a little louder this time, "Let her go."

"This may be a stroke of luck," Sameer says, without even seeming to hear me. He lets go of my arm, steps closer to Anu. "The failure of the bomb will disappoint the men I answer to. But if I bring them such a prize as this one," he says, tugging on her braid, harder this time, jerking her head backward, bringing his face closer to hers, "then all the better."

"You cannot—" I say, the words choking in my throat. I'm so enraged, my hand itching for the knife at my hip. I stare at his neck, want to rip it open, yank that gold chain he's wearing from it, see his blood spill out on the dirt. I've done it before, I think, killed a man. At least this time it will mean something. It won't be an accident.

"Quite right," he continues, turning his back to me, inching toward Anu. "Not before we've had our fun with her. Stand watch and we might even give you a turn—"

Enough! I lunge at him, releasing the knife from its sheath. The tip of the blade is at his throat and I wrap my other arm around his chest before anyone else realizes what's happening.

It is hungry, this knife, having waited long years since last being used for its intended purpose. A drop of blood rises up under the tip of the blade before I steady my hand.

I think of Arish. What would he say if he knew that this was the way I was using his gift to me? To protect a Sikh girl. And I think of my parents and worry for a moment that what I'm about to do will reach them.

They would want me to do the right thing. Even if it means killing Sameer.

But maybe I won't have to.

"Tell them to let her go," I whisper in his ear. And I pray to Allah that if the knife is not enough to scare him off, maybe what I am about to say will be.

CHAPTER 24

ANUPREET

No, no, no, no.

Oh. Hey Rabba, no!

Please.

Not again. Why is this happening again?

How?

But it is. And it's all so much like it was that day in the shop. The smell, tobacco on his fingers. The feel of someone so close, too close, close enough that the sweat off his chest is soaking through his shirt, through the back of my kameez.

Only, this time there is no Mr. Singh there to hit him on the head from behind.

Only Tariq.

Against three.

Tariq and a knife. Where did he get a knife? Oh, thank Rabba, he at least has a knife!

He keeps the blade at the one they call Sameer's neck, the point digging into his skin. Tariq's holding him like the big one holds me. But Sameer doesn't look afraid. I kick, try to scream, but the hand across my mouth is mashing my lips against my teeth and I can barely breathe let alone make a sound. "Let her go," Tariq is saying.

Yes! Let me go. I won't tell anyone. I don't even know what to tell. Just don't take me. Don't . . .

I can hear music from inside the house. Margaret's harmonium. Margaret! Margaret, come and look out the back window. *Look out the window!*

"Tariq with a knife," Sameer says. His voice edges higher, like he's surprised but not afraid.

I should have recognized Sameer from that day in the market with Manvir. I should have run before it was too late. Stupid!

Hey, Rabba. Please. Don't let it be too late. I'm sorry for all the times I thought Manvir and Papaji and Biji silly for warning me. Sorry for thinking they were being too cautious. If only you'll make them let me go, I'll listen to them always. I'll be careful.

Just don't let them . . . please. *Please.*

"I said let her go!" Tariq's voice grows deeper, almost a growl. He presses the knife a little harder into Sameer's neck. Blood seeps up from the wound. Tariq's hand is trembling.

He's as scared as I am.

We're both going to die.

I kick again. The one holding me clamps down harder. I can hardly draw a breath. My vision goes fuzzy at the edges.

"Consider, Tariq," Sameer says. "You may kill me, but one knife against three? Think on it, brother."

"I'm not your brother." Tariq's face is like stone. "And I won't need to kill you." He pauses, then adds, "You're going to walk away."

What?

Sameer laughs. "Walk away?" The others laugh as well.

Tariq is pagal. They won't just leave. Why would they?

I have to do something. I kick backward at my captor, trying to land my heels sharp on his legs.

The policemen—at the front gate—Rabba, make them hear us. Make them know something is wrong. Why won't Margaret stop playing? Why doesn't she come and look?

Please!

But no one comes.

Tariq swallows hard.

The knife stays locked on Sameer's neck.

"Even if you manage to kill me," Sameer is telling him, "and then go for one of my friends, the girl is sure to get hurt."

"Better she die than what she might suffer with you," Tariq says quickly. Unexpectedly, a wave of fury surges through me. I hate that dying is the only way some people can think of to protect a girl.

"You love her?" Sameer is smiling coldly now. "Is that it?" He looks me up and down appraisingly, then his eyes find those of the one who holds me. "He loves the little Sikh girl." Only he doesn't say *girl*, but something in Urdu that I don't understand but sounds so nasty on his tongue that I know enough of what he has called me.

"Let . . . her . . . go," Tariq repeats, but he doesn't deny it.

Why doesn't he deny it?

Tariq?

Me?

I think of his looks.

Of that day in the kitchen.

It can't be.

I've been scared of him. Everyone's tried to protect me from *him*.

It doesn't make sense. Nothing makes sense.

"Let *me* go," Sameer hisses, losing his composure for a moment.

"The girl first," Tariq says, adding quietly, "or I tell your friends how you come to have gold to wear."

There is only a moment where Sameer's eyes give him away. But I see it.

Fear.

The tiniest spark of it flashes there, eyes flitting sideways to try and get a look at Tariq.

"It's funny," Tariq says, almost whispering in Sameer's ear, "how some of the stores in the Sikh market weren't bothered during the riots last week."

Markets? This is how he will save us? I want to scream and cry and disappear. We're going to die.

But Sameer hesitates. "You talk of markets? You're off your head." But he doesn't sound surprised. He sounds . . . *worried*.

"Only, I thought you'd like to know," Tariq says carefully, "since I saw you shopping there a few days before."

Shopping? Hey, Rabba. Why doesn't he do something! Please, God, make him do *something*.

But what if he is? The one who's holding me is confused, too. His grip loosens a bit and he turns and asks the other, the one with his head shaved close, what Tariq is talking about. I try to kick free, but he grabs my braid, pulling my head back harder.

"He's off his head," Sameer says again, this time to his men. Then he says to Tariq: "You can't kill us all with one knife, and if we don't kill you where you stand, we'll carry the tale of what happened here to our brothers. Our *true* brothers."

Tariq narrows his eyes but holds the knife steady.

"I wonder, though," Tariq says, his voice dropping even lower now, so low I can barely hear, "who will these true brothers of yours kill first? Me? When all I've done to anger them is spoil one of their plans and then deny them a girl they may not even want? But you! You have more to answer for, haven't you? Maybe we should ask your friends here what happens to traitors who take—"

"Enough!" Sameer is livid, panicked. Spittle flies from his mouth.

"Tell them to let her go," Tariq demands.

Sameer looks at his gundas, maybe checking to see what they've understood. Finally, he nods.

And suddenly I'm free. I fall to the ground, land on my hands and knees, gulp air.

Thank you, Rabba. Thank you. Thank you.

Tariq is telling them to leave. I look up to see Sameer nod to the other two, and they move off uncertainly. I half crawl as I scramble behind Tariq and find my feet.

He waits until the others are out of earshot, at the corner of the compound before he releases Sameer, pushing him roughly forward so that he falls in the dirt. But Tariq keeps the knife extended toward him, ready.

"You are a dead man," Sameer warns, bouncing to his feet. "They will believe what I tell them. We will come for you."

"It will take time," Tariq says with a shrug. "Even you might find it difficult to explain how I convinced the three *brothers* to move off, despite the fact that I had only one knife."

"I will think of something," Sameer says, touching the smear of blood on his neck. "And you will lose everything."

Why do they stand here talking? I reach out, pull at Tariq's free arm. We should go. Run! But Tariq shakes his arm free, keeps the knife pointed at Sameer.

"I have nothing left to lose."

Sameer laughs again, "Nothing?" He gestures at me with both hands, palms up, as if offering me to Tariq. "It is for this *nothing* that you risk your own neck?"

"Go before I change my mind and call them back to tell them about your bribing. How you're keeping the money."

Bribing? Is that what he meant about the market?

Sameer backs up a few steps, curses. "Soon every true Muslim remaining in Jalandhar will know of your treachery! And if somehow you manage to escape to Pakistan alive, we'll find you there."

One look at Tariq tells me that Sameer is not bluffing.

And if he believes him, then it means what Sameer has said about him before is true. Tariq has already risked his life—once for Mr. Darnsley in bringing the bomb to the rubbish heap, and now again in helping me.

Sameer's two friends watch from the corner of the compound, the smaller one looking nervously up the lane.

"Sameer!" he hisses. "A sipahi!"

Sameer holds up a hand to his man, a silent order to wait. He glares at Tariq. "We will find you," he says. "*I* will find you."

Tariq doesn't argue, just stares back as he holds the knife out between them.

Sameer gives an odd little laugh and backs up another step, shaking his head. Then he turns and runs to join the others as they sprint up the alley and into the dusk.

Only then does Tariq let his arm holding the knife drop to his side.

They're gone. They're really gone. And I am still here. We both are.

I grab at his hand, pull. "Come inside," I urge him. Tariq nods. But he doesn't move yet.

"They'll come back, won't they?" I ask.

He nods again. It's nearly dark now.

"Chalo," I beg, letting go of his hand. I can't stay out here any longer. I head for corner opposite the one where Sameer disappeared.

He stays still. Why won't he come? "Hurry up!"

He looks at the knife in his hand, as if he is considering using it some other way. "He's right."

I want to scream at him that we must run, but I wait.

"My life is worth nothing now," he says, thumbing the knife's edge.

"No!" I snap. "Tariq—"

"I've nothing left," he says. "My plans . . ."

He stops. Looks at me. "I'm sorry."

Sorry? I shake my head. I don't understand.

"Truly," he says. "For all of it."

And I wonder what exactly he's apologizing to me for. Sameer? Or the bomb? Or that day in the kitchen? Or maybe for the train?

Whatever it is, it doesn't matter now. He saved me. He saved my life. "You are forgiven," I assure him, mostly to get him moving, to get us to safety.

I extend my hand. He looks at it a moment, his face going soft. But he doesn't take it. Instead, he walks over to the pile of rubble at the base of the wall. He moves one of the larger chunks of concrete, drops the knife behind it, and then puts the stone back.

He turns. "It served its purpose," he says. "My brother will be satisfied."

I have no idea what he means, but his hand is in mine now, and we're racing toward the edge of the compound, cutting our way up the busy lane to the front gate. Half a dozen policemen and our regular guard stand there. Two of the officers start to move toward us before the guard waves us by with a grunt. We hurry to the rear entrance of the house.

Margaret is upstairs, still playing the vaja. And I realize that she's been playing the whole time we've been in the alley.

Which means she saw nothing.

I tighten my fingers on Tariq's hand, drag him up the stairs and straight to Margaret before I can convince myself that I'm not doing the right thing.

She stops playing abruptly as we barrel into the room. "You haven't finished the job behind the compound already, have you?" she asks. Her eyes dart to our hands, still laced together. I release his quickly, let my arms fall to my sides. But something shifts in Margaret.

I shake my head, unsure now of what to say. "Nahi."

"Then what do you want?" she demands.

"Your father, miss," I say, adding, "we need him."

She rises to her feet. "We haven't been able to reach Daddy yet. He likely hasn't even reached Delhi. Mother phoned Radcliffe's residence to leave a message, and sent a wire to the viceroy's residence—"

I stop listening as I realize he cannot help us. And he cannot help Tariq from so far away, even if we could reach him by phone.

What are we going to do?

I look up at Margaret.

Her eyes tear up. She shakes her head. "He doesn't even know about the bomb. Not yet. He'd be here otherwise, with us. But Mummy says it's better that he's not."

She's worried about him. If someone tried to get to him here, they might try to get to him or the others in Delhi. I reach for her hand. She draws it back, crosses her arms, sniffs.

"At any rate, it's nearly done. The car will be back by dawn. Mummy and I will go. Pakistan gets independence tomorrow, India the next day, and that's all she wrote. Everybody will leave and everything will settle down and go back to normal." She's trying to convince herself. But she doesn't believe it. Neither do I. It's only going to get worse. For a while, at least. It will be a long time before anyone can get on a train and feel safe. There is no normal anymore.

But I can't do anything about that. Only Tariq can I do anything for.

"Madam?" I ask. "Can we see her?"

"Mother is indisposed. This afternoon's events and Father's absence resurrected an old habit. I had no idea you could scare up that much whiskey in this country, but Mother managed." Margaret leans against the bedpost. "She's useless until morning."

"She needs help?" I ask, confused.

Tariq mumbles behind me. "She means the mistress is intoxicated."

"Yes, the *mistress* is drunk," Margaret says. "Almost dying has a way of driving her into a bottle. She went through sherry by the pint during the blitz back home. So I'm afraid if there's something you require, I'm the only one who can answer."

Finally I speak about what brought me up the stairs.

"We need help, miss," I say quietly.

She chokes out a laugh. "Help? Oh, you two seem to have done quite—"

I cut her off. "Tariq is in trouble."

She waits a beat. "What kind of trouble?"

Tariq looks nervously out the front window at the guards, at the street, and I wonder if the shadows and silhouettes moving there look as threatening to him as they do to me. Every one could be Sameer and his friends.

"Please, miss, not so near the windows—"

She makes a face. "What are you on about?"

"If we can see out, then they can see in," Tariq explains.

Margaret is incredulous. "They?"

"Your father's office, miss? Please?" I beg, already moving for the door.

"What is going on?" Margaret demands, racing to catch up, reaching the office before me and opening the door. Once we're inside the room, she switches on the light on the desk, shuts the door behind us. The screens are still closed, the deep veranda blocking much of the view.

"Tell me," she demands.

"The bomb," I begin. "Tariq did . . . not."

She looks annoyed. "Of course he didn't—" But she stops herself. Her expression changes, washing through a hundred different emotions before she speaks again, eyes wide with surprise and understanding. "My window," she says. "That's what you were worried that I saw!" She begins to sound panicked now, takes a step backward. "You brought it here!"

Tariq steps forward, barks out a protest, but then I speak again. I don't know what makes me so bold. Perhaps it was almost dying twice in one day. Perhaps it is the debt I owe to him now, but something in me wants to make Margaret understand, to see if this one problem can find a way of resolving itself. "He didn't know," I say.

"It's true!" Tariq says. "I intercepted the parcel that was being delivered because I saw it came from a fellow I once knew. Sameer. His name is Sameer. We were at school together for a while, but he's taken up with some dangerous people. They meant it for your father. I just thought it was some kind of nasty prank, so I threw it in the rubbish before I came back inside. But had I known it was a bomb—"

Margaret's eyes go wide with shock, then they narrow. "Why should I believe you?" she asks. "You've been manipulating and deceiving since you arrived in this house. Scheming, plotting—"

"I believe him," I say to her.

She looks at me like I'm too simple to understand.

"Miss, this Sameer was here . . . just now." I tell her quickly what happened in the alley. Her face changes many times as she listens, wearing shock and anger and fury by turns.

"Is this true?" she demands of Tariq when I finish my tale. He nods.

"The knife?" she asks.

"My brother's. He brought it back from the war in Africa. It's in the alley now."

"Bells," she whispers, sinking into her father's chair. She presses her lips together, thinking. "These men," she says. "They will kill you?"

He nods. "They may have already killed Sameer if his friends have repeated what I said in the alley. At any rate, they will come for me eventually."

"Can't your family protect you? Friends?"

He hesitates, drops his eyes. "They have gone to Pakistan already. I stayed behind. . . ."

He doesn't finish. His family left for Pakistan? But why didn't he go with them? I look to Margaret—she seems to already know.

"Damned idiot," she says.

His silence offers agreement.

She exhales. "What do you think I can do for you?" she asks, but she doesn't sound angry anymore. "Go see the coppers."

"No!" he shouts. "They'll never believe me. A Muslim who remains in India while his family has gone on will be seen as one who stayed behind to make trouble. And tomorrow when the award is announced—"

"They will be even less inclined to offer protection to the likes of you," she says, her voice grim.

We're silent a moment. In the distance, thunder rumbles again. Rain—the real kind—is coming. Soon.

"We have to wait for Father to call," Margaret says, her voice strained. "I don't know what else to do."

I look around the room, at the piles of parcels and crates that we all spent the day packing, the lids not yet nailed onto the frames of the biggest boxes, and suddenly I have an idea.

CHAPTER 25

MARGARET

Anu darts across the room to the largest of Father's crates, the lid resting against the side. She studies the instruments, the stand for the transit, the leather cylinders capped on either end, dozens of maps rolled tightly inside. She crouches down to read the shipping information affixed to the lid. It is printed in English and Hindi, or Punjabi; I still can't tell them apart.

"This crate," she says, running a fingertip across the words printed in Father's careful hand. "When leaving?"

A popping noise from outside makes me jump, but it's only a motorcycle backfiring. I turn back to Anu. "Tomorrow. First thing."

She looks up at me, the question in her eyes.

Tariq understands before I do. "You cannot mean to send me to London inside a wooden box!"

Anu straightens. "Only Bombay—"

My mind races, thoughts vaulting over one another, but I force myself to think clearly. It's mad. But not entirely. Not entirely. "The crate goes overland to Bombay and then is loaded onto a steamer," I say. "It will be weeks before it reaches England." Anu is clever with more than just hair oil and dancing.

"I'll suffocate," Tariq whispers. But he does not panic, even now. "Or starve."

"Maybe not. And if what you say about Sameer is true, you're worse than dead if you stay here," I tell him.

Tariq hesitates, stares at the box as if he isn't so certain this is so.

"How many days to Bombay?" I ask him, trying to remember where it is on the map.

"By truck? Four, perhaps five with the roads as they are," Tariq says. "But the crate might be left sitting somewhere for days before—"

Anu surveys the chasm of the crate, says something to Tariq in Punjabi.

He hesitates, shrugs. "Haan."

"What did she say?" I ask, jealousy flaring up a tic that they can shut me out.

"She says I only need to be out of Jalandhar," he replies.

She really is dead clever, this girl. I pick up her line of reasoning. "You can get out of the box at any time after the first day or two and figure out from there what to do. Aren't there scads of Muslims in Bombay?" I ask him, wondering if word of his betrayal could spread so far. Somehow I doubt it.

He nods. "Yes. Much of the city. I would be safer there."

We look at the crate again, this time Tariq moving to its edge, peering inside, but he is still careful not to touch it. As if he is afraid. It is large enough for him to fit comfortably. Quite wide, and if he curls up his legs a bit, he should be all right.

"The instruments," he says, sizing up the crate, perhaps trying to figure out what it will be like to be nailed shut inside it.

"If we leave them in there with you, they'll end up busted. Or you," I point out.

I think of him in the box. Nestled into the straw, his delicate features protected against the bumps and jostles of the road. And I think of what Mother said of Anu: "If I could ship home a dozen of her, I would." I insanely wonder what Mother might do if the crate arrived in London with Tariq as cargo.

Even more insanely, I think that his appearance would surely, finally put to rest any harping on the subject of Alec. It's almost enough for me to want it to work. But I know it can't, of course, not to London. But Bombay . . . maybe.

"We move"—Anupreet scoops up the transit case—"to other crates." She deposits it in another smaller box nearby. "But this . . ." She lifts out the transit stand and surveys the other crates.

"It's too long," I say, looking at the other packing options, finding them all woefully small. "It can stay behind," I say, feeling almost giddy at the thought of doing this. I take the contraption from Anu, lean it up against the wall. "Anyhow, Father was always a bit stunned that his kit made it here at all. I think he'll be almost relieved if something takes a walk this time."

Anu rummages about in the straw, drawing out other items. Tariq, looking dazed, joins in. We work, pulling things carefully from the box. Soon a great heap of equipment litters the floor around us. We dig deeper, silent, listening to the noise from the street outside, the sound of the pack of guards at the gates laughing. Once or twice my hand brushes one of Tariq's or Anu's below the surface, swimming through the sea of straw. And it strikes me, oddly, that that they feel familiar. Like they could be the hands of anyone, that their color or beauty or scars are invisible to my own fingers.

When the job is done, I stand, look down into the box and try to imagine it as a cozy place, not just the best alternative to a violent death in the street. I try to picture Tariq sleeping there, like something in a fairy tale—Snow White under her case of glass or Sleeping Beauty in her tower. I try not to think too much about the practicalities like hunger or thirst or what he will do to relieve himself.

Or what he will do if the box really does go missing.

"Food and water," Anu says, pointing at the box. Again, I'm surprised at her quickness. And then a bit shamefaced at my surprise. How could I have thought so little of her this whole time? I was too busy trying to decide if she was my friend or my rival for Tariq. What a git I've been.

"I'll need a hammer or pry bar to let myself out," Tariq says, staring in despair at the box.

"Bit of luck that this one doesn't have a proper lock on it like the trunks," I offer. Bugger it all, but I've almost forgotten now how angry I was with him. The fury and embarrassment I felt a few hours ago seem so far away now. *We're not so different*, I reckon. After all, I'm no stranger to wanting things beyond my reach.

Plus, he saved Anu's life. And, yes, Father's. He saved my father's life. Tariq nicked the package from the delivery boy, made sure it didn't get into Father's hands, was the only reason the bomb didn't go off in the house, where it might have injured Mummy or me or one of the staff.

And I realize in a rush that he didn't have to do any of those things. All he had to do was *nothing*. It would have been easier for him. And the people who sent the bomb might have rewarded him for it in the bargain, too.

But he did *something*.

Then I realize with a shock that in protecting us, the little boy was harmed. Tears start at my eyes as I think that he might have seen the parcel, might have thought it was another of my little presents. Nausea washes over me again, but then . . . then! I realize that if he'd opened it properly, it wouldn't have been his leg that was hurt. More likely he stepped on it climbing over the rubbish heap. The thought doesn't give me much comfort, but I don't expect I deserve it, anyhow. I choke back my tears, yank myself together as Tariq asks, "But even if I make it to Bombay, what then?"

"Father has a reference for you," I say quickly, turning and going to the desk.

"He has given it to me already," Tariq says. But something else catches my eye.

The commendation Father received from Mountbatten.

The small brass medal is still in the case on the desktop, the letter on the creamy paper open next to it. I look at the signature on the page, the last viceroy's regal hand peaking and falling like the jagged outline of the Himalayas.

"This," I say, picking it up. "We can use this."

Tariq and Anupreet join me at the desk. "How?" she asks.

"Another letter," I say, staring at the signature, convincing myself I can make a go of forging it. "Another letter"—I hurry to the crate nearest the window, lift out the Corona typewriter, grab a sheet of paper, and feed it between the drums—"containing a reference and bearing the signature of Mountbatten himself."

Anupreet is nodding excitedly.

"You can find work, at least," I say to Tariq, adding, "all they'll need is a piece of paper with the viceroy's signature on it, and you'll have a job quicker than they can say 'Bob's your uncle.'"

I'm being a bit sunnier about the whole thing than it deserves, but the poor bloke will need something to hope for. Surviving the journey out of the Punjab will be the hard part.

Outside, the noise grows louder and I go to the window.

"What's happening?" I ask, catching a chorus of voices singing in the distance.

Tariq listens. "Early celebrations for independence."

Funny, but it doesn't feel festive. Not like it was in London two years ago when the war ended in Europe. That was a corker, it was. Dancing in the streets, parades, the whole bit. And everybody smiling at everybody else, Trafalgar Square all the way up to Buckingham Palace one solid river of people, all happy for the first time in years.

But I know it won't be the same out there. There's a pitch to the celebrations and the singing outside that makes it sound an awful lot like the riots of just the other week. The words of the songs may be different, but the tone is the same. No one is screaming, at least.

"So, peace?" Anu whispers the question.

"Until there isn't," Tariq says. And we all know what he means. The line between contentment and envy is thinner than any line on any map.

Lines are funny things. They make us feel safe—at least for a while—knowing where we end and something or someone else begins. But they can also make us want, can make us bitter, wanting what lies on the other side of the line. But whether it's a border on a map or a boundary between two people, the lines are still only lines. Still something someone made up, decided on. They're not even real, but so long as everyone agrees to play along, they work fine. But how can lines on a map tell a piece of land what to be any more than lines between one person and another can pretend to be what makes them different? I pause, then look from Anu to Tariq.

They are listening to the singing outside as it drifts away from the compound and begins to fade. And I wonder what that singing means to *them*. I've never asked.

I don't realize I'm holding my breath until I let it loose. "Well," I say, "we've work to do." I make to head back to the desk and the typewriter, start thinking of impressive things to say about Tariq, and impressive ways to say them. I wish I'd paid a bit more attention in my composition classes at school.

Tariq lays a hand on my arm to stop me. The touch is so natural and familiar, I feel strangely calm. He looks at my face, then Anu's. "Why do this for me?"

It looks as if it pains him to ask the question. And I wonder what he's done to Anu to make him so surprised that she would help.

"You saved my life," Anu says. It really is simple for her, this transaction. But I worry that if her family learns of the help she gives this boy, they'll see her as the traitor, like Tariq. I hope they never find out.

But he seems satisfied by her answer. He waits for mine but won't look at me. But the hand stays on my arm, fingers wrapped around my wrist.

Lightning flashes, washing the room in brief, white light. I hear the first giant drops of rain begin to fall.

"It's the first thing anyone asked of me since I arrived," I say, realizing how true it is as I say it. There's so much trouble here in India, will be even more now with two countries instead of one. But doing something—even if that something is as desperate as trying to save a boy's life by boxing him up and loading him onto a lorry—is still better than doing nothing, better than packing it in and bailing out, as Alec used to say. I suspect Tariq knows this, what with the way he protected all of us. And something tells me Anu's known it all along. Maybe I have, too. I just haven't had a chance to do anything about it, apart from leaving silly little tidbits for the beggar boy.

The rain is really falling now, drowning all other sounds coming in from outside. It feels different already, this rain. We've had showers off and on while I've been here, even thunder and lightning, but they never lasted. Everyone went on and on about how late the monsoon seemed to be coming. But I know without asking that it has arrived. There's something unmistakable about the way the rain sheets off the end of the roof, a curtain of water hiding us from the street, announcing its arrival.

We stand there watching, the three of us, for ages, it seems, the cool spray of water misting through the screens. I look at them standing there beside me. They look like they belong together, the two of them, both so beautiful in their own ways. It's a pity they can't be.

Will I ever hear from them? Will I ever know what happens to them after I leave tomorrow? Will they? I like to think about

Tariq starting over in some place new. Or maybe even making it to Oxford someday. Why not? Why the bloody hell not? He's smart enough. Maybe I can even bring it up to Father when we get home. Maybe.

And Anu? Will she be all right? Will those men come looking for her when they can't find Tariq? Mother said more than once that she'd take Anu home with us if she could. Maybe we should. But Anu wouldn't go. She'd never leave her home. She'll just have to be careful for a little while, until things settle. And she'll have her family to look after her. She'll be all right.

Please, God, let her be all right. Both of them.

Anu goes to see about food for Tariq's journey. Tariq follows to fetch more crates for the rest of Father's things. They don't tell me what they're going for, but I know all the same. It's useless now anyhow, trying to talk above the driving rhythm of the rain.

No matter. There's nothing left to say. Now there is only the work of getting Tariq across one of those lines on the map that maybe shouldn't even be there.

I settle in at Father's desk and place my fingers across the keys of the Corona. I can't even hear the hammers strike as they flip up into the ribbon and the paper, but it doesn't matter. In my head I'm hearing a new song, sung in the lovely, humming voice of the vaja. The rain is steady on the roof like hands on a tabla, perfect accompaniment as I play a new kind of song on this typewriter. A song I know I'll never repeat, never even hear again, but I'm dead sure I'll never forget.

AUTHOR'S NOTE

In 2005 I participated in the Fulbright Teacher Exchange Program, which sent me to Chandigarh, India, a city created after the partition. I loved my time there, fell in love with Punjabi culture and food, music and literature, and the Punjabi people themselves. All of those things I expected. What I didn't expect was the way this story would find me.

One day a friend drove us north to see Amritsar, and a little farther up the Grand Trunk Road to the border closing ceremony in Wagah. Wagah was a village that was bisected by the Radcliffe Line in 1947. Until 1999 the Grand Trunk Road was the only road linking India and Pakistan, and Wagah the only point one could drive between the two countries. Elaborate gates mark the boundary, dozens of colorfully dressed soldiers stand guard. And every night thousands of people gather on both sides of those gates to observe the lowering of the flags and closing of the gates between the two countries.

While the tensions between India and Pakistan remain very, very real, the border closing is something of a pageant. The soldiers put on wonderful displays—drilling and high-kicking and performing for the crowd. And the crowd participates: chanting, cheering, singing, both sides trying to outdo each other. The atmosphere is something like a sporting event, with both sides rooting for their teams, trying to make the most noise, all culminating in a carefully coordinated lowering of the flags on both sides.

Still, I couldn't help wondering what it was like before. How long did it take for the border closing to evolve into entertainment? How long before people stopped mourning the way the village had been cut in half, the country split in pieces?

So I began asking questions. Over and over, I ran into people who had stories like the ones you read in this novel. India in 1947 was an amazing place, full of possibility and hope and the new thrill of sovereignty after the British were convinced to give up the jewel of the empire. But it was a dangerous place as well. I heard countless stories that helped me understand that. And I was struck by how fresh the wounds of partition still were for so many people.

And I began reading. Books like Alex Von Tunzelmann's *Indian Summer: The Secret History of the End of an Empire* and *India Remembered: A Personal Account of the Mountbattens During the Transfer of Power* by Pamela Mountbatten, as well as countless websites and articles. The more I read the more I became convinced that there was another story I wanted to try to tell.

Finally, I began writing, attempting to capture the perspectives of three different people caught up in these events. The story is fictional, and while I've been as careful as I can to honor the events and people and places, my purpose was not so much to recount the history, but rather to let it live through the characters. To that end, there are note-worthy differences between this book and the events that inspired it.

First, the setting. I chose to set the story in Jalandhar because it is located in the Punjab near the modern Pakistani border. The trag-edies that take place in the story are ones that happened all over the Punjab and Bengal, but not necessarily in Jalandhar.

Second, the characters. While many historical figures are men-tioned in the novel, the principal characters—Tariq, Anupreet, and Margaret—are all fictional. Margaret's presence in the story was inspired by that of Pamela Mountbatten, who did accompany her parents, the last viceroy and vicerine of India. But the Darnsleys are purely my invention. There would have been many civil servants in India at the time, but sadly very few of them were cartographers like Mr. Darnsley. The work on the border was done remotely, overseen by Cyril Radcliffe and a committee composed of four men, two repre-senting the Muslim League and two representing the Indian National Congress. Predictably, the committee often ended up deadlocked, leav-ing Radcliffe—a man with almost no practical experience of India—the unenviable task of randomly deciding where the border should fall.

Third, people did begin moving even before the borders were finalized as they do in the story, but the greatest of the "population exchange"—the largest human migration in history—happened after the announcement of the Radcliffe Line. As the characters in the book indicate, violence and unrest increased in the days after the August 15 handover and after the border was established. In fall 1947 the first formal conflict between the two nations erupted into war over the Jammu and Kashmir regions. Three more wars followed. Tension still persists between the two countries, despite sharing so many common-alities and so much history.

That history is too complicated for me to try to do justice to in the brief span of these pages. Even estimates regarding exactly how many people relocated vary widely, most falling within the range of 10 to 14 million. Likewise, the exact figure regarding the loss of life is impossible to cite definitively, with figures ranging from 200,000 to more than one million people losing their lives in the months leading up to and after the partition.

There are plenty of reasons for the differences in these numbers—lack of accurate census data from the early 1940s, lack of cooperation and communication between India and Pakistan post-partition, and of course the confusion and chaos of the partition era itself. Ultimately, that range of numbers is more haunting than a definitive number might be. Because among the countless tragedies and casualties of the partition, perhaps one of the greatest is not knowing how many voices were silenced, how many stories were cut short and lost forever. I can only hope this story does honor to theirs.

GLOSSARY

ABBU—Father

ALOO GOBI—Punjabi dish consisting of potato and cauliflower

AMMI—Mother

AMRITSAR—Important city in northern India, and home to the Golden Temple, one of the most holy sites for Sikhs. At the time of partition, it was home to equal numbers of Sikhs and Muslims, and therefore sought after by both sides. It eventually was included in India.

BENGAL—State in eastern India. Along with the Punjab, Bengal saw the worst of the violence during the partition. East Pakistan (now Bangladesh) was carved out of Bengal.

BETA—Son

BEWAKOOF—Idiot

BHARA—Cousin

BIJI—Mother

BUDHOO—Stupid

CHAI—Tea made with milk, sugar, and spices

CHALO—Hindi phrase meaning "let's go."

CHANA SAAG—Punjabi dish made with spinach and chickpeas

CHAPATI—A type of flatbread, often used to scoop up food

CHOLERA—A bacterial infection of the small intestine, frequently contracted through contaminated drinking water

CHOLI—A blouse worn underneath the sari

CHURIDARS—A type of pant worn by both men and women in India. Churidars are cut wide and loose at the waist and upper leg, but fit very snugly over the calf.

CHUTIYAA—Mild expletive

CHUTNEY—Any of a variety of mixes of spices, vegetables, or fruits used as seasoning or as a condiment to Indian cooking

CURRY—Any of a wide range of traditional stewed dishes. Curries may be made with vegetables, meat, or both.

DARAUNA—Dangerous

DAADAA—Grandfather

DACOIT—A robber

DHOTI—Traditional male garment. A single piece of cloth wrapped around the waist and legs. Gandhi was often photographed wearing a dhoti.

DIWALI—The Hindu festival of lights. It is widely celebrated across religions in India, celebrating the triumph of good over evil. It also coincides with the Sikh festival of Bandi Chhor Divas.

DOGRI—Language spoken in portions of northern Punjab, as well as Jammu and Kashmir

DUPATTA—A long multipurpose scarf that coordinates with a salwar-kameez.

GANDHI—Important political and ideological leader of the Indian
Independence movement. His nonviolent protests rallied
millions to the cause of independence, earning him the title
Father of the Nation. He was deeply grieved by the partition
of India along religious lines. He was assassinated in 1948 by a
Hindu nationalist who thought him too sympathetic to Muslims.

GHADDA—Impolite word to call someone

GHEE—Clarified butter used in cooking

GIDHHA—Traditional Punjabi women's dance

GURDWARA—A Sikh house of worship

GURU GOBIND SINGH—Tenth of the eleven Sikh gurus. Was
responsible for formalizing many of the tenets of the Sikh faith.

HAAN/HAAN JI—Phrase meaning "yes"

HARAMZADA—Bastard

HARMONIUM—A freestanding keyboard instrument, played like a
piano but relying on reeds to produce the sound

HEY, RABBA—Oh, god!

HINDU—A follower of Hinduism, the most widely practiced
religion in India. There are upward of three hundred million
recognized deities in the Hindu pantheon, but all are believed
to be manifestations of Brahman, the guiding, creative force
of the universe. Hindus are free to pick which manifestation of
Brahman to worship.

IBALISA—Devil

IMLI—A reddish-brown fruit. Also known as tamarind, the sweet and
sour flavor is widely used.

JAMMU—A region of Jammu and Kashmir, the northernmost state
in modern India. At the time of partition, Jammu was a princely
state, meaning it was not under the control of the British. The

leadership was advised to accede to either Pakistan or India.
After settling with India, it became part of Jammu and Kashmir,
an area that remains a focal point of conflict between India and
Pakistan.

JODHPURS—Riding pants, similar in style to churidars

JINNAH—Muhammad Ali Jinnah, leader of the Muslim League
in India before partition, and the first governor general of
Pakistan

JUTIS—Traditional Punjabi shoe

KASHMIR—Like Jammu, Kashmir was a princely state in India at
the time of partition. Its borders are still disputed by India and
Pakistan.

KHANDA—The emblem of the Sikh faith. It consists of a double-
edged sword, a chakram (a round traditional throwing
weapon), and two kirpans with handles crossed.

KHANDAAN—Family

KHEER—Traditional rice pudding dessert

KIRPAN—The short, curved sword worn by Khalsa Sikh men

KITNA HAI?—Phrase meaning "how much?"

KURTA—Long shirt worn by men

LAHORE—Important city in modern-day Pakistan. Like Amritsar, it
was highly contested by both sides at the time of Partition.

LAKH—Unit of numbering equal to one hundred thousand

LANGAR—Traditional meal shared after a service at a gurdwara. All
are welcome to join, regardless of faith or background.

LOHE KE CHANE CHABANA—To chew iron pellets, i.e. to do the
impossible

LYCHEE—Fruit with delicate white pulp

MAJRA—Town

MARGH—Road or path

MOGHUL—Name given to the Muslim conquerors and empire that invaded India in the sixteenth century and controlled much of the subcontinent until the early nineteenth century

MONSOON—Rainy period falling between May and September

MOSQUE—A Muslim place of worship

MUSLIM—A follower of Islam, India's largest minority religion, and the majority religion in Pakistan. Islam arrived in the Punjab in the sixteenth century with the invading Moughul armies.

NAAN—Leavened bread traditionally cooked in a tandoor

NAHI—No

NEHRU—Jawalharal Nehru was an Indian statesmen, elected leader of the congress in 1929. He became the first prime minister of free India.

NILLA—Blue

PAGAL—Crazy

PAGRI—A turban worn by a Sikh man

PAISA—$1/100$ of a rupee

"PAKISTAN ZINDABAD"—"Long live Pakistan."

PALLU—Loose end of a sari

PANI—Water

PAPAJI—Father

PARATHAS—Flatbread cooked on a tawa

PARTITION—Name given to the separation of India from Pakistan

PATTHAR—Small stones

PUNJAB—Region of northern India and eastern Pakistan. Once united, it was the region most changed by the partition.

RAB RAKHA—Parting phrase meaning "May God protect you."

Ragas—Similar to scales in music

Raj—Means "reign" in Hindi. The British Raj refers to the period between 1858 and 1947 when the British ruled India.

Rangoli—Folk art patterns made on floors of homes to celebrate festivals and welcome Hindu gods. Rangoli are often made with colored rice, flour, grains, or flower petals.

Rickshaw—A sort of taxi used to transport people around. Cycle rickshaws are pulled by bicycles.

Rogan Josh—Spicy lamb dish

Roti—Bread

Rupee—Basic unit of Indian currency

Sahib—Master

Sal—A type of tree

Salwar-kameez—Traditional suit of clothing for Punjabi women. A salwar is a pair of loose-fitting pants like pajamas but gathered at the ankle. The kameez is a long tunic worn over the salwar.

Sambar—A type of deer native to South Asia

Samosa—A stuffed, deep-fried pastry. Samosas are often filled with some combination of spices, vegetables, potatoes, and ground meat.

Sari—Long strip of unstitched cloth serving as a garment for Indian women

Sat Sri Akal—Traditional Sikh greeting, roughly translated "God is the Ultimate Truth."

Shukriya—"Thank you."

Sikh—A follower of Sikhism

Sipahi—A policeman constable or military officer

Tabla—Traditional percussion instrument, consisting of two hand drums

TANDOOR—A traditional clay oven, often heated by a wood fire

TAWA—Large flat skillet used for cooking

TIFFIN—Light lunch

VAJA—Hindi word for a harmonium

VANARA—Shapeshifting creatures featured in the *Ramayana*, an ancient epic poem widely known throughout India.

VICEROY—A royal official who runs a colony or country on behalf of a king or queen. Mountbatten was the last viceroy of India.

WALLAH—Hindi word that can mean a maker of something or deliverer of something